CICADA

TANYA PELL

CICADA

KILLER VHS SERIES
BOOK 4

SHORTWAVE
PUBLISHING

Cover and interior design by Alan Lastufka.

First Edition published September 2024.

10 9 8 7 6 5 4 3 2 1

ISBN 978-1-959565-34-5 (Paperback)
ISBN 978-1-959565-35-2 (eBook)

For Doug who continues to road-trip down I-22 with me.

CHAPTER ONE

S he was going to kill Richie. She was. Before this fucking trip was over, one of them was going to die.

"Jesus, Ash, would you stop acting like a bitch for five seconds?"

Wind from the open window tore tendrils of hair from Ashton's ponytail, sending them slashing across her face like wicked little razors. But with no working AC, she had tried to suffer in silence. Tried. And God how she suffered. Still, Ashton sucked down a deep breath of hot, humid air laced with cigarette smoke from Richie's incessant chain smoking and forced herself not to scream or rage or slam her elbow into his temple. He was driving after all. Rude.

"I'm literally just sitting here, Richie," she said quietly, staring out the dirty windshield spotted with dead bugs, bird shit, and highway dust, the view beyond not much of an improvement, just empty fields and hills of scorched grass, trees packed together in places, and the shimmering blacktop of I-22. "I haven't said a thing."

"And you're being a bitch about it," her boyfriend mumbled around his cigarette. "You think you have to speak? You've got your face on."

"This is my face." To be fair, her resting bitch face *was* her face. But she also knew she was typically being a bitch. At least when she was around Richie. At least for the last few weeks.

They were *supposed* to be on this stupid idea of a road trip to have fun and get back to the way things used to be. Loud, crazy sex in sleazy motels. Greasy pizza and gas station Slurpees. Buying (stealing) shitty souvenirs from random hole-in-the-wall tourist traps in each state. More loud, crazy sex behind state signs along the highway if possible.

So far, the trip had been greasy pizza, Slurpees, fighting, accusations, and slammed doors. Not exactly a full bingo card.

Richie mumbled something unintelligible. And probably unintelligent, she wasn't going to split hairs. She glanced at him sidelong from behind her cheap, pink, plastic heart sunglasses snagged from a convenience store in Georgia. Richie had his shirt off, his lean, wiry muscles on full display, as was his happy trail of curly, coarse hair along his belly that was more skin than either muscle or fat. His greasy mop of hair was damp against his temple and obscured her view of his eyes. His sloping nose and high cheekbones she still found attractive were unobscured, and his thin lips were—like always—wrapped around one of his no filter cigarettes. His right hand gripped the steering wheel, his arm covered in black and grey tattoos. Barbed wire around one wrist. Nautical star at his shoulder. Old English letters that had bled so badly along his inner arm that they might have said RIP WALKER or COCKSUCKER.

Probably the former since Walker had been Richie's dog as a kid, but she could have made an argument for the latter.

Ash asked herself for the millionth time what she saw in him. They'd met at a Disturbed concert. Her initial impression of him was that he was foul-mouthed and way too cocky for someone with a jaw you could break with one good punch, but he'd been funny and flattering and they'd had fun for a while. But then his jokes had started to become condescending and his flattery directed at anyone who wasn't her.

When he'd told her about a Nu metal music festival in Texas and suggested a road trip, she had thought it was a sweet, hokey gesture. She'd actually gotten excited. Austin had a pretty decent reputation for its music scene and the festival featuring both classic bands like Korn and debut artists she'd gotten pretty obsessed with. Even convinced herself Richie was making the effort.

Now they were on a seemingly endless highway in Mississippi with no AC, fighting for the fiftieth time since breakfast and it wasn't even noon.

"Shit."

Ash opened her mouth to ask what his problem was with her *now*, when her eyes focused on the road ahead and she realized Richie was probably not referring to her.

His old Camaro slowed and then came to a gear-grinding halt behind a minivan. Beyond that, miles of highway completely gridlocked. In the distance just beyond an overpass, black clouds of smoke billowed, lights from emergency vehicles reflected against the mass as if it was solid.

Without the wind blowing through the windows, the already vicious heat struck Ashton with the force of a hammer blow. Her tank top was already plastered to her skin, and she imagined how attractive she looked with her boob sweat and under arm stains. Her butt was clinging to the seat in her cut-off shorts. She wanted a shower. And food that didn't come out of a crinkly bag. And a new boyfriend.

Great. She was stuck in the middle of fucking nowhere in bumper-to-bumper traffic with no AC and she couldn't stand her boyfriend. Yes. Way to go, girl. Your *Eureka* moment could not have come at a better time.

Maybe she would just catch a plane home. Screw the cost. Bail was way more expensive.

"This shit goes on for miles!" Richie griped, as if she couldn't see that for herself.

Ashton beat down the urge to retort with a witty *No shit, Sherlock* and instead clamped her lips shut, reaching for her phone charging in the center console. One bar. Enough to map a new route maybe. She tapped maps and watched as her phone tried to find a satellite somewhere up beyond the haze of sepia sky. The long red line that appeared along their route was not reassuring. She tapped a bit.

"I don't see any exits coming up."

"Then what the fuck is that?"

A couple of miles ahead, an old off ramp came into view, a van in worse shape than Richie's Camaro making its way slowly up the faded concrete to come to a halt at the intersection before it crossed the bridge turning further South.

No signs. Not even a mile marker. She enlarged the area on her phone. "I dunno. It's not on here."

"Well, it's good enough for me," Richie said pulling onto the shoulder, gunning it down the rumble strips so the car bounced and shook rhythmically.

"We have no idea where it *goes*," Ashton said through gritted teeth.

"That van probably mapped an alternative route already. We'll just head that general direction. And it's better than sitting here with my dick in my hand. Unless you—"

"No. Thanks."

He shrugged, pushing his hair back with his spindly fingers. Sweat had matted the hair under his arms into a solid piece that looked like an old toupee. His hand came away slick from his damp head and the moisture glistened on the worn steering wheel as he regripped it. "We'll probably find a way around. Besides, I need a piss and we're gonna need gas."

Ash shifted in her seat. She also wanted the bathroom but had mostly driven it from her mind. But now by mentioning it, the pressure on her bladder had returned in full force. Still, she wasn't sure. . . "It's probably a closed road to nowhere. Or to a town full of mutant psychos with banjos."

He gave her a shit-eating grin. "If only you played the banjo! You'd fit right in."

Ash bit the inside of her cheek, stowing her phone. Yes. Before this trip was over, he was going to die.

CHAPTER TWO

Ash slammed the car door a little more than was necessary, picturing Richie's skull cracking as the door met the frame of the car, the sound of metal on bone. She didn't really know what metal on bone would sound like, but she imagined it would be satisfying and crunchy.

They had been driving for over half an hour down looping roads, passing nothing but abandoned gas stations and boarded up houses, roofs caving in, doors warped in their frames. They'd lost cell service miles back. But Richie had refused to turn around, his hands clenching so hard on the steering wheel that only self-preservation kept Ash from manifesting him snapping it off and sending them spiraling into a tree.

"I swear to all that is holy, Richie, you are the single most stubborn asshole I have ever had the displeasure of—"

"Whine a little harder, Ash. Please. It has been so fucking helpful so far," he said, coming round the back of the car, yanking an old, faded black t-shirt over his head, the arms cut off. He popped the gas tank door and twisted off the top, leaving it swinging against the car to yank the fuel pump from its cradle.

Ash ground her molars, hearing them squeak in protest. She was going to need dental work if she kept it up. In order to save what was left of her fraying patience and precious teeth, Ash stormed across the oil and fuel-stained lot to the no-name gas station. At first, Richie had taken it for just another pile of bricks and planks left to fend for itself, but Ash had spotted the red neon sign in the window. OPEN. She'd yelped and he'd slammed on the brakes so hard she'd had to brace herself. She had a suspicion he'd done it deliberately, especially as he'd muttered the weakest of apologies as he smiled around another fucking cigarette.

She yanked open the door to the gas station, a tarnished, silver bell tinkling dully above her head to mark her entry. The space was cluttered, like most tiny stations. Spinning displays of sunglasses and metal shelves packed with garbage food meant to survive the apocalypse, magazine covers faded from being hit by the dying sun day after day, and plenty of oil, wiper fluid, and WD-40. Aerosol sprays of Lysol were stacked next to old bottles of Febreze and those tiny tree air fresheners that smelled nothing like pine. Along the walls were coolers, the doors smudged with fingerprints, the lights inside flickering on and off, illuminating in flashes the bottles of water, energy drinks, and sodas. A sad coffee machine was in one corner, stained brown and black. In another corner—

"Yes," she breathed between chapped lips. A bathroom sign.

She made a beeline before she was stopped by a voice behind her and she nearly jumped out of her skin, squeezing her legs together and momentarily wondering if she had just peed a little.

"You'll need a key, dear heart."

Rounding, she saw an old lady at the counter, nicotine-stained fingers and teeth, leaning on her elbows in a high back chair, one cigarette caught between two upturned fingers as if she was a femme fatale in an old noir film. Her Coke bottle glasses made her eyes appear buggy and massive, dwarfing her other features. Except for her hair. Her hair was teased and twisted in an old beehive, grey and white with long strands of what might have been brown, glistening slightly as if it had been shellacked with an entire can of Aqua Net.

Behind her, a taxidermy armadillo squatted on a wooden base, its armored plates and snout covered in dust, cobwebs dangling between its ears. A little golden plate attached to the wood read *Jerry*. Jerry's tiny eyes were so obscured by dust, he might have had cataracts, but Ash couldn't help but feel like he was aware of her.

The old woman reached beneath the counter and pulled out a rusted hammer, its handle covered in electrical tape, a key hanging from the cord looped through the bottom where a hole had been drilled. She slid it across the counter.

"Thank you," Ash said, rushing forward.

"Tha's alright."

Ash wrapped fingers around the handle. Someone had written The Shitter across the rusted head in permanent marker, bringing her up short in surprise. The woman made a sound in the back of her throat. "Hood-lums. But ev'ry time I change the key, someone does something else. I don't even bother none, anymore." She shook her head and Ash noticed her hair didn't move at all. The old woman looked out the window toward the car and Richie at the pump. "You can always tell hoodlums."

Ash's face flushed with heat, but could she really fault the old lady for being perceptive? Richie had more than a few chips on his shoulder, and while Ash didn't go around looking to start trouble, she certainly didn't mind finishing it. The lady had probably seen them yelling at each other in the lot and pegged them as foul-mouthed twenty-somethings that refused to grow up. And maybe Ash was tired of that, too. Still, what right did a stranger have to judge her when she was obviously tired, sweaty, and had a shit-for-brains boyfriend to deal with?

"Thanks for the key. I'll bring it right back."

Walking quickly away, Ash could feel both Jerry's and the woman's eyes tracking her through the small space, past the aisle of trail mix, beef jerky, and boxes of raisins wrapped in cellophane. Ash gripped the hammer harder, thinking that it was a stupid sort of item to attach a key to if you were so worried about 'hoodlums.'

At least the bathroom was clean.

Ash peed and washed her hands and face. Even wiped down her arms, neck, and collarbone with damp towels. She finger-combed her hair and rebound it into a floppy bun on the top of her head and smoothed her eyebrows with wet fingers. She felt a little better with some of the sticky sweat and dust off her skin. Would feel even better when she could get some proper food.

Maybe she'd despise Richie a little less?

But as she emerged from the bathroom and he was standing there, leaning against the door with a face that would freeze beer, she didn't hold out a lot of hope for that last thought.

He brushed past her. "Finally. Thought you'd fallen in."

He let the door shut in her face and hadn't even bothered to take the key. She decided not to make a scene, hated looking like 'the crazy one' in public. And Richie was *so* good at pushing her buttons quietly enough so when she finally lost it, she always seemed the villain.

Ash walked the key back to the counter and offered up a wan smile, determined to be courteous. "Thank you."

The lady put the hammer back under the counter. "Y'all lost?"

"I'm not really sure. We got off the main highway and there's no service. Do you have any maps?"

A grin cracked the old woman's face, the skin of her cheeks folding and creasing into lines and hollows. "Didn't think youngins even bothered with 'em anymore. They're there," she said, gesturing with her cigarette.

There were several old, folded maps of Mississippi and Alabama, some of the Natchez Trace and a couple of big, old atlases so yellowed she wondered why the woman even kept them stocked. Half of the roads within had to be gone.

She snapped up one of both Mississippi and Natchez,

just in case. And she did a small circuit of the store, grabbing sunscreen, and a water. She hauled her purchases
up to the counter, passing them over and digging out
some cash from her pocket. Her eyes fell on a bunch of
lighters in a box marked at three dollars. They were just
plain Bics, but they'd been hand painted. She lifted her
glasses to better see. A bug, its bulbous eyes red and
round like two beads, had been painted on the plastic
surface. Its wings were transparent, veined with black
and green.

"I'll take this, too," she said impulsively, liking the
strangeness of it. "As a souvenir. Did you paint these?"

The old woman shook her head but rang up the total.
"Bless your heart, with my eyes? No, but the artist is
local. Y'all should head into town. Festival's today."

"What festival?"

"The Cicada Film Festival. Folks made a movie round
here a few years back."

"Yeah? What movie?"

A finger dotted with age spots pointed to a rack in
front of the register, the whole thing full of VHS tapes.
Ash hadn't even noticed them. The cover was black and
green with slashes of red. A bug, similar to the one on the
lighter, but creepier, took up most of the space, staring
out at Ash. *CICADA*. A horror movie? Weird. And on VHS?
Weirder. Who even used VHS these days?

As if in answer, the woman continued. "Yeah, you
could only watch it on tape. Low budget sort of thing.
What do they call it when it is a bunch of people running
around in the dark? And you're supposed to be watching
what happened to 'em?"

"Found footage?" Ash said, looking at the bleeding letters and red, bulging eyes of the insect.

"That's it. They got the whole town decked out. And it is the right time for it too. Cicadas waking up this time of year." She tsked. "Imagine spending almost your whole life underground only to die just as you really start to see the world. Mmm mmm. Just makes you count your blessings."

"They got food?" Richie said, sidling up behind Ash. "I could go for a McGriddle."

The old woman eyed him cooly. "No chains. Only local fare. But it's a damn sight better than anything out of a common drive-thru. They'll take good care of you. Visitors get special treatment. I recommend Hey, Sally's for a late lunch. Biscuits are handmade and you get 'em fresh as you sit down."

"Gimme a pack of the Lucky Strikes. Unfiltered," Richie said, pointing behind the register.

"Son, I'm not gonna give you shit. You can ask for them as if your mama put effort into raising you right. I recommend, 'Ms. Dottie, could I purchase some cigarettes from your fine establishment?'" She said Ms. like Mzz and Ash had to bite back a shit-eating grin.

Richie clucked his tongue and angled his head, as if he might stare Dottie into submission, but the old woman didn't even bat an eye behind those Coke bottle glasses. Just held her cigarette between her fingers with a look of disdain that said Richie was less than the skid marks he had on his underwear. Richie, seeing he was getting nowhere, scoffed and headed back out.

Dottie took a drag on her cigarette, watching Richie

swagger to the car and slam the door. He waited all of two seconds before he lay on the horn, apparently his new mating call. "Like I said. You can always tell a hoodlum. You get in that car, girl, you deserve what you get. That one's already marked."

A sound that was part agreement, part annoyance escaped Ash's mouth. Like she had any other choice? "Yea, well," she said, annoyance winning out, "it's him or hitchhiking and at least with that one, I don't have to worry about things getting any weirder."

Dottie coughed, a wet sound from lungs and windpipe coated with tar, handing over Ash's purchases in an unmarked plastic bag. "You'd be surprised."

As the door closed behind Ash, Dottie's parting words were almost drowned out by the old bell's clanging.

"Y'all have a lovely day!"

CHAPTER THREE

I t was no small torture going from the sweet, sweet air conditioning of the gas station into the boiling heat outside, the steady hum of insects in every direction. Maybe a summoning. Maybe a warning. Goosebumps pimpled Ash's arms in total contrast to the temperature, and she tried to wipe them away.

She felt exposed. She wanted to run, which was ridiculous on several fronts. 1) She hated cardio. 2) What would she be running from?

"Are you gonna take all day?" Richie snapped.

Oh yeah.

Ash rolled her eyes behind her glasses, refusing to rise to the bait. She just needed to get to Texas, and she could be done. Okay, she was done. *So* done. But she could be free. Hell, maybe she wouldn't even wait till Texas. Maybe she would just wait for the first Greyhound terminal she saw.

She slid back into her seat, knees angled away from Richie. Code for 'don't fucking touch me.' Richie didn't give two shits about her signals because he was peeling out before she even had her seatbelt fastened, taking the left into town. Which was fine, Ash decided, cracking the seal of her water bottle to take a long drink. Maybe food would put them both in a better mood.

She doubted it, but maybe. Stranger things could happen. See? She could look on the bright side. And her mother thought she was a pessimist. A pessimist with horrible taste in men. Okay, fine. She'd give her mom that one. Fair was fair.

A sign rose out of bleached grass outside her window, the wooden posts chipping white paint. REVELATION, it said in big, green letters. Like the book of the Bible? She was a lapsed everything, so she couldn't be sure. She wrinkled her nose, hoping they weren't heading into the tightest notch on the Bible Belt. She wasn't against religion or faith, but she wasn't so sure "hoodlums" would be very welcome, festival or no.

Though it was somehow the birthplace of an underground horror film.

As Richie roared toward Revelation, taking the turns too sharp and doing very little to avoid the potholes that covered the narrow stretch of road through a forest thick with conifers and oaks, Ash spread one of the maps on her lap. Absently, she reached forward to turn the music down.

"What are you *doing*?" Richie asked.

"Looking for where we are?"

"Why do women always need to turn down the music so they can see better?"

"I would explain concentration to you," she said, keeping her tone bored, "but you'd likely lose interest before I could even get started." Which was the case in so many situations. She found the last exit she remembered before leaving the highway and started searching around for a town called Revelation. She checked the index and finally found it, using her finger to trace the grid.

Her brows knitted together, finger following the road they traveled on the map. Revelation was bordered on three sides by a vast forest. The road went into town but did not go through. To get back to the interstate, they would have to backtrack the entire way or go round.

"I don't think this shortcut is very short, Chief," she said dryly. "It looks like—"

Richie turned the radio back on, music blaring from the speakers, drowning out her voice.

First. Greyhound. Terminal, she swore. She would not spend a minute longer in Richie's company than necessary. At the first sign of real civilization, she was out. Dottie was right. If she stuck with a loser like Richie, she deserved anything she got. To avoid arguing, Ash went back to studying the map, marveling at just how many places there were in and around the Natchez Trace to hide a body.

The drive was only a few minutes, the trees giving way to a pristine little main street running straight into Revelation. It was like driving onto a movie set. Maybe for a *Back to the Future* reboot. All the shops on either side of the road were little mom-and-pop stores. A hardware store. A grocery. A couple of restaurants. Even a movie theatre.

The light poles were all garlanded with dried flowers. Ash doubted real flowers would have survived long in the sun, and it was actually rather pretty. A big banner stretched right across the street from one building to another, painted with two dancing bugs, welcoming them to CICADA FILM FESTIVAL. Hokey, but cute.

As they reached the end of the street lined with people mingling about the shops, cones and a uniformed officer directed them to a lot beside a laundromat filled with out of state plates. Richie slowed to a stop as the officer approached the driver's side window, eyes obscured by mirrored shades.

Richie grumbled and turned down the music as the officer leaned down, big fingers curling over the lip of Richie's window. "Afternoon! Y'all in town for the movie festival?"

Before Richie could offend, Ash flashed a smile, seeing herself reflected in the cop's glasses. "We got a bit lost. Dottie from the gas station? She told us about the fair."

"Oh, it's more than a fair, miss! You'll see! We've got everything. But you say y'all got turned round?"

"Are we being interrogated, officer?" Richie said snidely.

The man turned his head slowly and Ash didn't have to see his eyes to know he was giving Richie the once over, fingers digging in just a little deeper to the worn interior of the door, tan knuckles whitening. "Not at all. Just glad of visitors. New faces are always welcome. Just like to know if folks heard about our little town. Helps the Chamber of Commerce plan for the next festival. And we just want you to have a good time!"

He stood back and Richie drove into the lot, Ash watching the officer's head follow the car in. "Do you have to be so rude to absolutely everybody?"

"Do you have to flirt with absolutely everybody?" he countered.

"What the actual fuck, Richie?! I didn't even remotely—"

Richie adopted a high, nasal whine. "Oh, officer! Please! Would you like to frisk me and—"

"You're unbelievable."

He snickered, pulling into an empty spot. Ash gathered her sling bag, checking to make sure she had her wallet and purchases from the gas station inside. Shoving the door open, she nearly slammed into a parking attendant.

"Whoa!" The attendant, a heavy-set woman with close cropped hair and dark skin put a hand to her heart and laughed in surprise, taking a step back so as not to crowd. Her long, dangly earrings tinkled musically. "Sorry if I scared you, hon! I just wanted to give you your map and coupons!"

"Wh-what?" Ash said, dumbly, holding out her hand for what the woman offered.

"We give 'em to e'erbody so you know what is happening when. Itinerary is right inside." She then pointed toward the main street. "If y'all want a bite, all the restaurants are that way. We've got some stands in the center of town, too. Lots of local wares. Fun picture spots for couples. There's the forest tours, which I recommend personally. Always nice to stroll through the shade and stretch your legs after being in a car for a spell. There's screenings all day of *CICADA* in the theatre and, child, what a relief from the heat! And the fireworks are extra special this year! You won't wanna miss those!"

Ash unfolded her own map. "Actually, I was wondering if this was accurate. It looks like there is only the one road in, and I wanted to know if there was a quicker way back to 22."

The lady pulled her lips in and shook her head. "'Fraid not. Past the square is only the residential area."

"Oh."

"You poor thing. You look worn out. You head on into town and into one of the restaurants and air so you can rest and get you something to eat. Too thin. Youngins today are always too thin." She patted Ash's hand, squeezing gently.

Ash tried to conjure a smile. The woman seemed genuinely kind, eager to help. Sure, she was probably trying to keep them so they'd spend money, but Ash was gonna take any little kindness she could get. Even if it cost her.

CHAPTER FOUR

Another car eased into the lot. "Oops! Gonna get replaced if I don't get back to it, hon," the attendant said as she pulled back with a cheery wave.

Ash held up the glossy map she had been handed. A postcard style picture of the town's main street was emblazoned on the front. She opened it to a cartoon map of the town with yellow roads surrounded by green forest that made her think of the Wizard of Oz with the same dancing cicada from the banner in each corner.

Wiping a hand across her forehead, already sticky again, Ash wondered at the going rate for souls because she was very close to considering offering hers for a shower. But maybe demon deals were best made on a full stomach. "That restaurant is right around the corner. The one that the gas station attendant mentioned. Do you wanna go there?"

Richie was sucking on a cigarette, cheeks hollowed out. He looked worn and Ash actually felt a little bad for how much they were fighting. "Whatever," he said, coughing a little, smoke clouding the air around him.

When he didn't move, she tried again. "Should I go on ahead and get us a table?"

"I said, 'Whatever.' I'm finishing this first."

She felt a little less bad.

She stalked across the blacktop, weaving between cars, looking back to see Richie pull out his phone and start swiping his thumb around on the surface. A familiar prickle of annoyance struck her. She'd seen the texts. She wasn't an idiot. Well, she *was* an idiot, but she wasn't ignorant. For whatever reason, she'd let herself get roped into this road trip thinking it would fix things. It had made them worse. And, even though she had already mentally checked out of the relationship, it stung to think he was also ready to jump ship. That he actually had another ship on standby.

He had obviously forgotten the lack of service because she watched him scowl at the phone, holding it up high above his head as he sought a signal. She could see his mouth moving around the cigarette, mumbling curses most likely. Good. Piece of—

"*Shit!*" Ash yelped as she rounded the corner and slammed right into someone, sunglasses falling to the cracked sidewalk.

"Sorry," came a low, bass voice that was more of a rumble than anything else. "You ok?"

Ash blinked, gazing up, up, up. Well over six feet tall with dark hair, curling and coiling round his ears and over his forehead was a man plucked from the cover of those old romance novels her mom used to read, complete with dark, sleepy eyes, full lips set in a lopsided smile, and a solid jaw. Actually, everything looked pretty solid from where Ash was standing, all muscle and smiles compared to Richie's angles and scowls.

"Huh?" Ash said, staring and unable to stop.

His smile only grew, as if he was used to such behavior. She would have bet all of her worldly wealth—which was admittedly not much—that he was. He leaned down, down, down to pick up her pink glasses from the sidewalk. "Sorry about the collision."

Ash tried on her own smile. "I'm pretty sure I ran into you. So, I'm sorry." She wasn't. She was not sorry.

He shrugged those giant shoulders. "Do we trade insurance information now?"

Was he flirting with her? This man, who looked like God had not so much as broken the mold as shattered it completely and declared creation perfected, was flirting with *her* when she was sweaty, gross, and still *technically* in a relationship? And was she thinking about flirting back? Yes, yes she was. Maybe the universe was throwing her one.

"I thought you were getting a table."

Dammit, universe!

Those sleepy eyes shifted from Ash to over her shoulder where she could smell Richie's cologne of funk and cigarettes as he eased up behind her. He threw a possessive arm around her shoulders, tickling her with the sweaty wad of hair in his pit. *GROSS!*

"I'll watch where I'm going. Sorry again," the guy said to Ash, shoving his hands in the pockets of perfectly fitted jeans before strolling past. She was sorry, too. So, so sorry.

"Like I said," Richie drawled, arm still round her shoulders as if it belonged there.

Fighting suddenly felt like a great idea. She hadn't flirted with the cop, and she hadn't flirted with the perfect specimen just then. She'd *wanted* to flirt with him, but Richie had ruined it like he did everything else. "Whatever," she said lamely, throwing off his arm and rushing ahead, needing space.

She had to step into the street to avoid more collisions, the sidewalk packed for such a small town in the middle of nowhere. Everybody was taking pictures or laughing. Having a good time. Jerks.

A striking girl in her early twenties was standing in the middle of the road, talking and gesticulating excitedly at a phone mounted on a tripod in front of her. After a minute, she tapped a button, grabbed the rig, and moved into the shade, shaking out long dreads, some dyed turquoise, pink, and russet, woven through with colored lace and wooden beads that clicked against each other. Her crocheted crop and low-cut shorts showcased a lot of warm, brown skin and she looked so effortlessly put together. So cool. She used a bamboo towel on her forehead, dabbing at the sweat beaded against her hairline, checked herself in her front facing camera before again taking up position in the street.

A vlogger or an influencer, then. Ash turned away just before she ran headlong into a light pole draped with more of the dried flower garlands she had spied from the car. They really were pretty. She liked the look of them, the long, gathered stalks of dried grass interlaced with fluffy, pink pampas and preserved lavender.

On closer inspection, she saw seed pods and twigs used to make crude bugs. She touched the wings of a cicada crafted from helicopter seeds, listening to the soft, papery crinkling. She used to throw them around the yard as a kid, chasing them as they spun and fell.

"You like 'em?"

An elderly gentleman was sitting on a bench in the shade of a hardware store behind her and she pointed to the garland and the little cicada. "They're very pretty."

The old man gave a lazy nod. "The ladies from the Rotary Club make 'em. You can buy 'em right at the center of town. Think they are set up near the fountain. Big white tent. Did Annaliese give you your map in the lot?"

"Annaliese? The parking attendant? Yea." She waved the map.

"Yes, ma'am. That'll show you where everybody's set up." The old man leaned forward, putting one hand to his ear. "You hear that?"

People talking. Motors. Foot traffic. The sound of a small town. But underneath it all—or maybe overtop—a steady hum of noise. The same buzz of insects from outside the gas station.

"Cicadas. *Thousands* of 'em. They stay burrowed underground for years and years, drinking from roots with their straw mouths. *Sluuuuuuuuuuuuuuurp!*" He sucked wetly through puckered lips. "A probiscis. That's what it's called. And they just live buried in that dirt until they crawl their way out and climb up trees to latch on and start moltin'; sheddin' that outer layer. That ex-O-skeleton. You're hearing the adult males. That buzz like an electrical hum is them callin' around. Fascinatin' stuff. Livin' almost your whole life underground and then comin' out after almost twenty years just to sing and breed and die. The pine forests around Revelation has the world's biggest population of cicadas. People like us? We keep 'em safe."

Something about the conversation was making her uncomfortable, like how she felt on edge outside the gas station.

"Right over there is where they're playin' that movie all day." He pointed a wobbling finger across the street where an old marquis displayed CICADA on both sides. Ash could see the walls covered with framed movie posters of the same VHS cover from the gas station. A bunch of people were filing in, some wearing antenna headbands or red googly eye goggles, most in black or horror movie t-shirts. "You seen it yet?"

"No," Ash admitted. "Never even heard of it before today."

"Well, you're in for an experience then." The man sat back with a chuckle, laying a finger on the side of his nose and tapping. "You go on and have fun, darlin'. And you tell 'em at the Rotary Tent that Mr. Danton said to set you up with the prettiest garland they got."

"Okay," Ash managed. "Thank you."

Ash continued on towards the restaurant, throat dry. A strange sense of unease swirled in her belly, but she chalked it up to hunger and heat and the incessant drone of the insects drilling into her brain.

CHAPTER FIVE

Hey, Sally!'s was easily spotted, the sign yellow and friendly, showcasing a buxom woman in a gingham apron holding a steaming plate of biscuits.

Upon entry, Ash was immediately assailed by glorious air conditioning and the smell of fresh, buttery biscuits. A long wraparound bar, the front a red, white, and black tile mosaic, took center stage in the room, red padded stools bolted into the floor. Vintage neon signs and hundreds of license plates covered the walls. A pristine jukebox held court off to the side, tucked in among the booths and tables. Littered across the ceiling were a few old television sets with the built in VCR, all on mute, all playing the same film. Something with jerky camera movements and all the quality of a home video. The *CICADA* film, she reasoned.

"Hi!" A pretty blonde woman appeared at the hostess stand. "Table for one?" she said merrily, painted red lips stretching wide.

The door opened on Richie's signature hacking cough. Ash reluctantly held up two fingers. The woman gathered two menus and two rolls of utensils, leading them to a table near the front window, pouring them each a glass of water, those red lips still too wide. "Y'all enjoying the festival?"

"We just got here," Ash answered. "But Dottie at the gas station said this was the best place."

The woman cooed. "Oh, Ms. Dottie, bless her. She sends everybody to us. You look over the menu and I'll be right back with your biscuits!"

Ash quickly chose the turkey club before sitting back, trying to relax, but the discordant hum of conversations took on a faint roar like the sound of the insects outside. . . .

"Do you have any service? I still can't get a signal."

"It is just like the original film!"

"You think any of the original cast will be here?"

"Oh, yeah. I've probably seen *CICADA* a hundred times."

Her gaze drifted to the walls and all the license plates. A few Mississippi. Some Alabama. But most were further out. South Carolina. Pennsylvania. Even California and New Mexico. And they all had a logo over their tag expiration sticker. A cicada.

"This town is wild for this bug," Ash mused aloud.

The hostess showed up just then with the promised plate of biscuits. "Here we go! Honey, salted butter, and apple jam alongside!" she said sweetly, smile frozen and eerie, little flecks of red lipstick on her teeth. "And here's Amy! She's gonna take good care of you!" The hostess side-stepped as a teenager sidled up, paper and pen in hand.

"What can I get you?" Amy asked, chipper and perky.

Richie ordered a hamburger, onion rings, and a Dr. Pepper. Ash gave her own order. Richie dove into the biscuits while Ash only nibbled even though it was buttery and soft, and the apple jam was one of the best things she'd ever tasted. She had the festival map next to her plate, glancing over the schedule of events. None of it mattered since they'd be on the road soon after lunch, but she'd rather read than talk. It was safer for everybody.

The food arrived soon despite the crowd, and Ash didn't even try to fill the silence, just tugged her other map out of her bag and again tried to make sense of a route, eating her sandwich without even tasting it. She found herself looking around for someone watching her. She couldn't rid herself of a nagging sensation, like they shouldn't be there because *of course* they shouldn't be there. They were supposed to be on I-22, but Richie had all the patience of a toddler.

And all the manners of one, she thought as he reached across and grabbed fries off her plate without asking. "Well? You've been staring at that map forever. Now what?" he mumbled around a mouthful of *her* fries.

Ash pulled her plate closer, bristling at his tone. Even if she did feel there was something not quite right about the place, she had already decided it was her against him and saw no reason to commiserate. "There is only the one road back to the highway. So, we either go back the way we came and hope the on ramp isn't blocked or go alllllllllll," she drew a circle round the forest with her finger, "the way around. If you had just listened in the first place and not gotten off the exit without any plan—"

"That's one of your biggest problems, right there," he said, cutting her off while crunching an onion ring, grease glistening on his teeth and lips.

Oh. There was a list. This would be a fun game. She considered all the witnesses and opted not to reach for a utensil but a fry. Chewing, she propped her elbows on the table, folding her hands under her chin, eager for the wisdom she was sure Richie was about to bestow.

"You're uptight."

She nodded as if it made perfect sense. "My attempts to find a route to the highway make me uptight."

"It is your constant fucking need to be in control of every situation. If things don't go your way, you can't just roll with it. You can't just be adventurous or have fun." He dunked his burger in the ketchup, sending a wave of red goo over the edge of his white plate where it dripped slowly onto the table into a thick puddle.

Ash counted to ten and shoved her hands under her thighs where she wouldn't be tempted. "Richie," she said calmly, "I can be adventurous. I can have fun. I enjoy fun. But when you spend half the trip trying to goad me into arguments and the other half of the trip texting your latest Tinder match, you can't really make a case for fun."

He almost choked, chewing and waving his burger at her, pieces of tomato and lettuce falling to the plate. "Do you hear how crazy you sound? I already told you a million times I've been texting my brother."

"I didn't realize Ross liked being called a dirty slut."

A muscle jumped in Richie's cheek, but he just eased back. "God, you really are ridiculous, aren't you?"

Her nails dug into her thighs. "I saw the texts, Richie. You aren't subtle."

"You didn't see shit. You're just delusional."

Ash shoved herself up till she was leaning over the table, feet planted, fingers like claws. *"You fucking lying piece of trash! I—"*

"Ma'am," said a gentle voice at her elbow. Their waitress back for refills. "There are kids around."

Richie sighed, his face a mask of disappointment and resignation. "Ash, come on," he said gently, moving to place his hand over hers.

She snatched it back before he could touch her, hissing like a cat, seething with rage. And though it made her feel defeated, she grabbed her bag and fled.

CHAPTER SIX

Sunglasses in place, arms crossed, not interested in making eye contact or small talk with anyone, Ash marched down the street. She managed to avoid hitting anybody or anything as she made her way back in the direction of the car, but she was fairly certain it was because everything leapt out of her way for fear of her wrath. She was not a bitch to be messed with and she made sure her face read, "FUCK RIGHT OFF."

She checked her phone with desperation. No bars. No WiFi. No hope.

It didn't matter she had stormed out of the restaurant like a child. It didn't matter she had let him twist things so she looked crazy *again*. What mattered was she was in the middle of Nowhere with no cell reception, no patience, and no fucks to give!

She rounded the laundromat, thinking she might just sulk in the car when she remembered it reeked and the leather seats would cook her legs. She'd have to find somewhere else to cool off. Fuck Richie. If he left her, good riddance.

The conifer forest loomed ahead, the dark spires of

the pines reaching up into the sky, turned to black tipped darts. The guided hikes. She'd do that. It would be nice and cool under the trees. People on the Internet—yogis and motivational Instagrammers with aesthetically perfect grids—were always saying shit like, "Go touch some grass," as if this was the solution to every problem.

Headache? Go touch some grass.

Hate your job? Go touch some grass.

Dating a dick? Go touch some grass.

She'd go touch some grass. Or at least walk in the woods. She was pretty sure the two were synonymous in this situation.

As she made her way to the park, she saw the parking attendant bending between cars, checking her phone before looking around, seemingly for a car. She did this dance two or three times, bending and pulling something from her pockets. She wasn't leaving flyers or anything on windshields and parking was free. So, what was she doing?

Maybe Richie was right. Maybe she was uptight. *Ugh.* Just the thought of Richie being right about something made her feel gross. Richie was still a liar and as useless as a crocheted condom and if she stayed with him she was likely to end up with a venereal disease or prison time.

You get in that car, girl, and you deserve what you get. Dottie's words from the gas station floated back to her. *That one's already marked.* Marked as what?

"Stop it," she told herself as she passed the square filled with huge tents selling all kinds of local wares. The big tent in the center was easy to spot, decorated with the dried flower garlands. There were two huge black and red canopies covered with those cheap, rubber insects hawking merch devoted to that weird-ass *CICADA* movie. Cheesy posters, bug faces on sticks, copies of the VHS. Still VHS? No DVDs? How stuck in time was this town?

The entrance to the guided trail was marked by a sign and she made a beeline for it, shoving her sunglasses to the top of her head as sun turned to shade. The thrum of cicadas and other insects was louder here in the trees, and she was grateful she didn't have to live with it all the time, tickling her eardrums and settling into the back of her skull, putting her on edge.

Or maybe she was always on edge. Maybe she really didn't know how to enjoy life without being in control. She kicked at a toadstool with her Vans, knocking its head off, the white, round ball dotted with tiny tumors sent skittering ahead before hitting a post and shattering into fragments of sponge. A sign marked the trail, a rope hanging across the path, blocking the way, a little wooden notice telling her the next walk would start at three thirty.

She'd missed it. "Dammit!" she said to the bugs in the trees, nails biting into her upper arms as if they were the only thing holding her together. She forced herself to withdraw her claws, rubbing her fingers over the tiny, crescent indents she'd made in her own flesh. You know what, fuck it. It wasn't like it was private property, right?

Ash stepped over the rope with ease and headed down the trail, sounds of the festival fading as she walked between the trees, pine needles like a carpet on both sides of the path. It was easy going, the way packed hard over the years. Craning her head back she could just see the tops of the trees high, high above her head, twisting spires of a natural cathedral.

Shutting her eyes, she listened to the rattle of the cicadas, a choir of clicking that seemed to vibrate the very air around her head. Ash found her shoulders relaxing, a smile touching her face. She inhaled deeply, tasting pine on her tongue like the purest gin complimented with the loamy, earthy smell of soil and damp wood. It was nice. So different from the thick, dusty wind pouring through the car or even the recycled, Freon-tinged air of the gas stations.

There might be something to the whole 'touching grass' thing.

Many of the smaller conifers were half-dead, trunks thin, their reddish-brown needles hanging from limp, drooping branches. Their bigger brothers and sisters had choked them, stealing the sunlight—leaving them to wither—while they grew full and lush. The breeze blew through their tops, stray needles and the random cone dropping from the canopy like a gentle summer rain.

It was all very dreamlike. A perpetual twilight had claimed the forest, putting Ash in mind of old fairy tales. The creepy ones, like Hansel and Gretel or Little Red Riding Hood. Not like she believed in witches or wolves. Well, she believed in wolves, but not like *talking* wolves plotting elaborate murder sprees dressed in drag.

Her fingers trailed across the bark of a tree, feeling the rough scales and the moss growing in thick, pillowy clumps along the trunk. She circled it, ferns and tall grasses brushing against her bare legs, tickling the back of her knees.

A few steps further and she encountered an intricate spider's web spun between two arching branches. It sparkled with tiny drops of dew yet to burn off in the heat of the day, the shade too thick. Small, pearly white clumps dotted the gossamer strands. The day's catch bound in silvery threads to be consumed at the spider's leisure. The spider was nowhere to be seen. Perhaps taking an afternoon nap.

Her nostrils flared as an odor reached her nose, tickling the fine hairs there. Rot, but not the rot of wood or leaves, but meat. Morbid curiosity had her ducking beneath the web and pushing at the fronds, careful of snakes.

The smell was stronger now and the buzzing of flies filled her ears. A swarm hung low to the ground, hovering over something. A patch of gray and red and white. Ash had to cover her mouth with her hand and take shallow breaths, the smell of death perfuming the air and threatening to overwhelm her gag reflex.

It was a racoon. Or so she thought. It was kind of hard to tell. The creature had been ripped apart, ribs protruding from the chest cavity, some broken into jagged shards. Its jaw hung open, teeth stained pink, gums receding, a swollen, purple tongue falling to the side. The bowels spilled out from the jagged hole in the belly, tubes of purple and blue muscle lying in a tangled heap. Maggots and flies and ants crawled across the surface, feasting upon the offal. The creature's eyes were gone, leaving empty holes of black shadow.

Ash told herself the dead thing was not looking at her. It could not look at her, being both dead and without eyes, but the brain is a funny thing, and it registers eyes where it knows eyes belong. It sees eyes even where they do not belong. And, even if it doesn't see eyes, it sees acknowledgment.

Ash was known. Not by a dead maybe-racoon. But something in the woods knew she was there.

CHAPTER SEVEN

Once you effectively scare yourself, it is good practice to laugh off your fears. Standing in the woods next to a dead something which may or may not have once been a racoon (or cat?) did not seem an appropriate place to laugh. Ash decided it was best to make fun of herself back on the trail. Putting her hand against one of the pines, she heard a faint crunch, yelping as she yanked her fingers back.

A bug. She'd touched a bug. She shuddered, hoping it wasn't planning on stinging her in retaliation. But her mind already registered the sound and texture as too dry, too crisp. She leaned in and realized it looked like a bug, but it wasn't. Well, not anymore.

The shell was almost completely intact, save for a thin line along the back that looked so precise it could have been cut by a scalpel. She could make out the head and the eyes, the tiny legs and ridges along the belly and back. A husk. The same shape as the cicadas all over town. What had the old man said? They burrowed out of the ground and climbed up onto a tree or a bush to shed their skins.

"Ex-O-skeleton," she remembered, mimicking the old man's drawl.

Annnnnnd she was talking to herself in the woods staring at a bug's discarded skin while a dead animal was decomposing only feet from her.

There was a rustle in the underbrush. Ash leapt back and away from the sound, but instead of landing on something solid, the ground beneath her just. . . gave way. Too soft. Too spongey. Looking down, Ash found entrails curling round the edges of her shoes. The head of the once-maybe-a-raccoon-but-might-have-been-a-cat turned stiffly along with the body as her clumsy feet disturbed it. Empty eye sockets stared up at her accusingly, like she had added insult to injury. But then the fumes hit her nose and the gnats and flies swarmed her face. Waving her arms and sputtering, Ash darted away from the death and decay and the barren husk of something soon to die, feeling her stomach churn. There was all manner of ick on her shoe and her club sandwich was threatening to escape back the way it had gone.

Away. She just had to get away. She would walk a bit further and then circle back to the main trail, giving the dead and whatever lurked a wide berth. She tried to pull in air through her mouth, the tingle of rot still lingering. Her shoes. Damn it! She slid her foot back and forth across a root covered with ivy, trying to scrape any of the remaining fluids and gore from her Vans.

Wait. What kind of ivy was that? Kudzu. Just kudzu. Not poison ivy. Right?

"OMG I *just* wanted to touch some fucking grass!"

Still talking to herself out in the woods after having

stepped in a pile of dead thing and now she was going to be eaten by mosquitos and may have just rubbed herself against poison ivy. Things were great. Nature was awesome. She should do this more.

"This is fine," she said, the words a puff of air against her lips. "I'm just gonna get back on the trail. And I'm going to stop talking to myself now."

Neither of those things turned out to be true. After a couple of minutes of walking, Ash had yet to find the path. "Fuck you, you stupid trail!" She supposed she was actually talking to the trail, but it probably didn't care much. Or it was hiding out of spite. Ash could almost believe it. She operated quite a bit on spite, why wouldn't the trail? Or the woods themselves? Hell, whatever had killed the she-was-still-not-convinced-it-was-a-racoon hadn't eaten it, so maybe it had been killed out of spite. Such thoughts occupied Ash's mind as she walked. Did animals murder each other or was that purely a human thing? Animals killed over things like food and territory and mates. Wasn't that kind of murder-y? Was murder-y a word? When did she get so *morbid*?

She was trying to distract herself from the plain and simple fact she was lost. The conifers grew denser, their tops reaching dizzying heights. She passed a tree struck by lightning, the inside hollowed out, black, charred wood still visible all along its trunk. It had burned from the inside. Another empty husk.

Ash rubbed her arms, willing away the psychosomatic tricks her mind and body were playing on her. She did not feel spiders in her hair. She was not covered in mosquitos. There were no eyes watching her. She needed to think of something—anything—to take her mind off how scared she was starting to get. She was not lost in the woods. Nobody got lost in the woods these days!

"If you go down in the woods today, you're sure of a big surprise," she sang, something in her brain triggering the old song. "If you go down in the woods today—"

You'd better prepare to die.

"Jesus, brain! What is *wrong* with you?"

Before she threw her Hail Mary, she palmed her phone once more. Nothing. Which meant there was only one course left. She was just going to yell for help. She was fed up and her pride could just go right ahead and get fucked. Richie could laugh at her all he wanted 'cause his opinion mattered fuck-all anyway, so she was going to stand right there and yell for help. Just pick a direction and start screaming.

Orienting herself in the direction of where she thought Revelation lay, Ash opened her mouth to yell, but stopped. A tree stood just a little alone, like the rest of the forest was giving it a bit of a berth. A huge growth distended from the trunk, the top just slightly above her own head. It was brown and strange, nothing like the bark of the tree itself.

She stepped closer, wanting a better look because her curiosity was as much of a bitch as she was, obviously. As she neared, Ash saw the growth was some carving of a massive cicada husk. It was just like the one she had touched earlier, only *so* much bigger. The head was slightly more humanoid in shape, but the giant eyes still protruded, round and globelike. The artistry was incredible, the wood shaped and painted to look like the dried parchment of an exoskeleton. Thick leg stalks were stuck to the pine bark seamlessly.

Ash instinctively opened her camera app and snapped some pictures. Backing up to get a shot of the forest behind, she nearly fell into a hole, pinwheeling her arms to keep her balance. Someone had dug a huge pit near the tree straight down into the earth.

"Huh." She looked at the cicada and then back into the hole, thinking maybe it was a tourist spot. Guides probably brought groups of people on nature walks to take pictures with the big bug. A local nature geek would show how cicadas buried themselves and tunneled out after years and years before they crawled up a tree—just like this—and latched on.

But why was there no path? Why carve something so meticulously and beautifully horrifying in the middle of the woods?

And why was it so quiet?

It took Ash a moment to realize she could only hear herself breathing, too hard and too fast. It took her a longer moment to recognize what was missing was the hum of the cicadas. Like an ambient noise you only miss when it is gone. You don't realize just how loud it is until you don't hear it, its absence making you slightly uneasy. Or a lot uneasy in her case.

Ash licked at her lips, approaching the carving on the tree. But as she reached out a hand to touch a spot along the spine, she had the same feeling of being watched as before. Arm extended, fingers poised to touch, Ash froze.

She stared at it for what felt like minutes. Lids wide.

Eyes going dry. Nothing happened. But, just like the okay-maybe-it-really-was-a-racoon with its empty eye sockets, she felt known.

"Fine," she said aloud to the carving and the woods because they were never going to tell on her and, even if they did, she would deny it. "Richie was right. I am—"

It moved.

Ash was too terrified to scream, but not so terrified she didn't snatch her hand back as if burned. Something had moved inside the husk. It *was* a husk. It was not a carving. A jerk from within what was most certainly not a carving.

She didn't scream.

She ran.

CHAPTER EIGHT

Logically, Ash knew she was running in the woods with no real sense of direction, and this was not the wisest course of action.

But logic be damned.

Ash knew what she had seen. Sort of. She was a little hazy on just what in the actual fuck it really was, but she knew it wasn't supposed to *be*. That was not a normal thing! You were not supposed to find linebacker-sized cocoons in the middle of the woods with something presumably linebacker-sized inside it!

Somehow, her brain's instinct toward self-preservation kicked in (better late than never) and she remembered entering the woods on the left side of the square and the layout of the map. She remembered where the sun was when she walked into the trees. And, thank Jesus, the direction her feet were carrying her seemed to be toward those things and *away* from whatever she'd seen.

She tuned out all sounds, afraid she would hear the crack of branches, the whatever-it-was pursuing her hotly. There was nothing but her heart in her ears, pounding to the steady beat of *RUN, RUN, RUN*. So it was with some surprise when she stumbled quite literally onto the trail, nearly missing it in her mad dash.

Correcting, she fled downhill, only by some miracle not falling flat on her face. Skidding so wildly, round a corner, she had to lower her center of gravity, sending dirt and pebbles in a cloud of dust and scraping her hand as she reached out to a nearby tree to stay upright. Two men in athletic shorts and moisture-wicking tees were coming up as she was going down. One of them wearing blue Nike's the same color as his shirt, leapt off the path and into the brush, yelling at her to slow down before she broke her neck.

But she couldn't slow down. Couldn't respond. She needed to get away.

She could see the whites of the festival tents and in any minute the thing was going to wrap its spindly legs around her waist and haul her back into the woods because that's what *always* happened in horror movies. But it didn't and as she reached the low hanging rope, she leapt over it like a hurdler and kept running out of the woods!

And directly into the same man as earlier.

She sent them crashing to the ground in a tangle of limbs, the breath knocked out of both of them. Well, Ash was wheezing and panting because she was terrified and not at all athletic. As she looked down into those dark, hooded eyes from earlier, now narrowed in annoyance, she couldn't even form another weak apology.

The annoyance faded instantly to be replaced by concern. And even though she had hit him hard and sent him sprawling, he sat up and took her gently by the arms, pushing her back slowly. His mouth was moving, but she couldn't hear him over her attempts to pull air into her lungs. He looked around and finally slung her arm over his shoulders and carried her into the shade, snatching her water bottle out of her bag's pocket.

His mouth moved again.

Huh? she tried.

"Drink." She caught that one. Supporting her back with one hand, he tipped the bottle to her lips. As soon as the water touched her tongue, she tried to latch on, to drink greedily, but he pulled it away. "Slow. Try to take a deep breath for me."

She liked the way he said, "For me." She watched him take a deep breath and tried to mimic him, willing the panic that had replaced the blood in her veins away. She was safe. She was in the open with lots of people around and there was a very attractive man sitting with her.

He picked up her wrist and placed two fingers to her pulse. "Are you hurt?" He said it cautiously, studying her face and her reaction.

Ash opened her mouth to talk, but her teeth started to chatter, and the sound was enough like the damn cicadas that she shut her lips tight. She was still shaking and couldn't seem to make herself stop, so she wrapped her arms around her knees.

"How about we see if they have a medic tent?"

She shook her head, squeezing her knees together and dropping her head upon them, still trying to calm the adrenaline coursing through her system like a party drug. Her skin felt too sensitive, and she wanted to crawl right out of it. Was she in shock? Did she need a blanket? She hoped not, she was so sweaty. But she was cold, too. Was that shock?

She had just seen a giant bug thing in the woods. She deserved to be in shock.

"Can you tell me your name?"

Gorgeous guy was still talking. He wasn't touching her anymore, and she kind of would have liked it if he was. Not just because she wondered what he looked like without his clothes on, but because he was another person and he radiated safe, and she really wanted safe in that moment. She tried to answer, but her mouth was as dry as a cotton ball and she looked at the bottle in his hands. He gave her more water. It was lukewarm, but good.

Finally, she felt able to manage real words. "Ashton. Ash."

He smiled, showing off a great oral hygiene routine. "I'm Callum." There was a hint of accent in his voice that made her head go all fuzzy in a pleasant way. "Ashton, do—"

"Ash."

"Ash," he corrected. "Was someone chasing you?"

"I saw something. Out there," she said, pointing past the trail in what she thought was the general direction of the thing on the tree. "It wasn't. . . I don't know. . ."

Callum's gaze followed her finger and he stared into the woods. "You saw something? Like an animal?"

His tone didn't suggest she was nuts, but it was *just* on the edge of 'is this girl in her right mind' to raise her hackles. She pinched the back of her thighs, telling herself she didn't need to argue with the man who was trying to be nice to her just because she didn't like the inflection of his words. "No. Well, I don't know. I went into the woods and I got turned around and I found this *thing*. On a tree. It was like a big cicada thing."

"A cicada?" Now there was a tone. He looked around at the festival in full swing, people meandering around the tents. Callum dug into his pocket and pulled out a keychain he had obviously just purchased, the tiny, hand-written price tag still attached. "Like this?"

He held it in his hand. A brown cicada husk trapped in resin; the dome as smooth as glass. She recoiled even though it was as tiny as the one she had almost crushed.

"Yes," she squeaked. "Only big! Like, your size!"

And there was the face to match the tone. Callum shoved the keychain back into his pocket. "Was it maybe someone dressed in a costume? Or one of those cutouts like they have over there?" He jerked his thumb behind him, and she saw a big, painted cicada with a hole where the head might be, the movie title emblazoned across the bottom in letters meant to look like blood dripping. A kid had her head through the hole while an older woman— her grandmother maybe—fussed with a cell phone, trying to work the camera.

"No!" Ash insisted, pulling out her own phone and thumbing the photos icon. "This!"

He shielded the screen with his big hand and his eyebrows dropped. Finally, a reaction she could work with!

"It moved!" she explained.

"Moved?"

She did not like the way he kept repeating her every time she relayed new information. It was not indicative of belief. "Yes. Something was inside, watching me! Bugs should not be this big! And I *know* that sounds crazy and I know I look crazy right now, but I'm not and—"

"Okay, okay!" Callum said, holding up his hands, palms out. "I never said you were crazy. You don't seem crazy. You do seem overheated and scared. I think we should look for a medic tent and have you checked for heatstroke."

Which was just a nice way of saying she wasn't exactly crazy, but the heat had cooked her brain.

She spoke through gritted teeth, seeing red. "I was in the woods. In the shade. I was not hot when I saw this. I'm only overheated *now* because I fucking bolted after it tried to get me!"

"It tried to get you?"

"Stop repeating me," she snapped. "Sorry. Sorry." She blushed. "Okay, no. That was an exaggeration. But that doesn't change any of the other facts." She held up the phone again. "You see this, right? Like, you recognize that it not normal?"

He blew out a long breath. "Maybe—"

"Are you really going to mansplain?"

Callum sucked on his teeth and then huffed a laugh. "No. I rather like all my extremities where they are."

"Thank you." Ash clutched her phone, sliding through the images with her thumb, back and forth. There was no way, right? And it hadn't come after her. But still...

"Are you sure I can't convince you to go to a medic tent?"

"What are you? A doctor or something?"

"Fire marshal and volunteer EMT."

Her lips quirked. "Are you saying you're trained in mouth-to-mouth?"

His own lips turned up at the corners. "I have a card and everything."

He was flirting with her. Something told her that if this was truly a horror movie situation, she would not be dumb enough to be sitting near ground zero flirting with the hot male lead, so it was obviously *not* a horror movie situation, and she was paranoid like Richie said.

Oh, shit. Richie. Right. Fuck.

Wait. She owed Richie no allegiance. He certainly hadn't shown her any. And she had already made up her mind to ghost him at the first town not caught in a time warp. But maybe she shouldn't rebound before she had even broken up with someone? Was it even a rebound if you were just flirting with a stranger?

"You doing better? 'Cause we can see if this town has a doctor who doesn't still use leeches or the word 'hysteria'."

She nodded, smiling thinly. "Yea. And I'm sorry for running into you. Again. And for being a bitch." He said nothing. "This is the part where you say I wasn't being a bitch."

He scrunched up his face. "Kinda were."

"Fair."

He smiled and it was lopsided and she felt hot all over again. "It's alright. I like it."

"You like crazy bitches?" Hot damn, she had news for him.

"I thought you said you weren't crazy."

"Don't argue with me."

"Yes, ma'am."

She could get used to this.

A pair of familiar Chuck Taylors appeared between them.

Dammit, universe!

CHAPTER NINE

"Here you are, babe."

Babe? She was really going to vomit now. All over Richie's shoes.

Ash rotated her head to glare, wondering how in the world she could ever have taken his cocky smirk and overblown sense of self-confidence for anything even remotely appealing. Especially as he stood over her, grinning down with flecks of onion ring on his teeth and a knowing look in his eye. Like he had just caught her with evidence of some heinous crime, and he was considering how best to blackmail her. Or worse: humiliate her.

She really, *really* hated him.

The insight was very freeing in a way.

Callum looked to Richie and then her as if trying to make sense of the situation.

Me and you both, body.

Buddy. She meant buddy.

"What is going on, Ash? You freaked out the whole restaurant," Richie said, all fake concern.

Oh, he was good.

Callum frowned and she wasn't sure if it would be

better to take the offensive or defensive. She hated how quickly she could be perceived as either whiny bitch or crazy bitch. Because these were the only options Richie left her. There was no way to fight fair out of a corner when the entire room was boobytrapped by the biggest booby she had ever allowed in her pa—

"Do you think you could drink some more water?" Callum asked. An innocent question that managed to ground her.

"Yea," she said, choosing to ignore Richie.

"You sure I can't convince you to see a medic? Heatstroke is no joke."

"A poet, too?"

Callum smirked and managed to make it look endearing instead of snarky. "I can't claim credit for that one. But I am pretty sure the ones who drop out of training either can't handle the blood or the bad jokes. Blood doesn't bother me, and I love bad jokes."

They were growing on her, too.

"Heatstroke?" Richie interjected, all pretense of concern gone. "Seriously, Ash, are you so desperate for attention?"

Callum's eyes went hard as stones and his jaw set so firm she was positively sure it was granite. She had an inspired flash and a scene unfoldeded on the movie screen in her brain. Of Callum jumping up and challenging Richie. Of a brawl breaking loose as her honor was defended. Callum was somehow shirtless and in those tight riding pants and tall boots looking very much like a beefy, sweaty Mr. Darcy.

While Callum didn't leap up or have a costume

change between blinks, he did turn his head on his corded neck—seriously, how many muscles was he smuggling?—to regard Richie with a flat stare. "Dude, give it a rest. You're not helping."

Her boyfriend shuffled back and forth nervously. Richie was a tool, but he wasn't completely void of intellect. Without anybody to back him up or any clear getaway, there was no way he was going to be able to start a fight and not end up needing someone with Callum's emergency credentials when he ended up broken and bleeding on the sidewalk.

Satisfied Richie was quite finished, Callum looked at her sympathetically. "You gonna be okay?"

"Yea. Thanks."

He stood, offering a hand to help her up. She took it, letting his palm swallow hers. His tug was gentle, and he even steadied her when her knees wobbled a bit. "Alright then. Take care."

Before he could disappear, she squeezed his hand. "Callum?" Richie seethed and she loved it.

"Cal. I usually go by Cal."

"About what I saw? Maybe I'm wrong, but I don't really think this is the best place to stick around, you know?"

He didn't smile or tease her, but actually seemed to. . . listen? A novelty! "No worries. I think I'm gonna head out soon, too."

"Okay."

"Okay."

They stood there awkwardly for a moment longer before Cal slipped away, head angled down toward his feet. Ash watched him go, trying very hard not to feel sorry for herself.

"Wow, Ash, were you just gonna blow him right in the middle of the park?"

There was a time—about an hour earlier—when Ash would have screamed and berated Richie for being an asshole. But none of those things made any difference to him. They only served to make him more of an asshole. At this point, she was pretty sure they had completely gone beyond what ass there could be, and he was only hole. A black hole of joy she had the unbelievable bad luck and worse judgement to fall into.

Instead of losing her temper, she just sighed wearily and started walking back to the car. "Of course not. I would have at least moved to the perimeter of the park. There are kids around."

Back at the car, Richie slammed the door, slammed the gear shift into reverse, and probably would have crashed into another vehicle, had someone not blared their horn. He let out a string of curses toward the back window, flipping the other driver the finger, and floored it out of the lot at the first opportunity, causing people to leap out of his way.

Richie didn't say anything as they made their way back along winding curves and kudzu covered trees. Ash had a very distinct feeling he was angry she hadn't given him the satisfaction of an argument rather than because he was actually jealous. Well, there might have been some of that, too, she thought, preening a bit. But more importantly, Richie had made a fool out of himself and hadn't been able to goad her.

As soon as they were back on the highway and back to the world of cellphone reception, she would Google the nearest bus station or even airport on her map. She should have asked Cal for a ride. He seemed normal. Oh, sure, so did a lot of serial killers, but how many of them were *that* hot?

Ted Bundy was hot.

Shut up, brain! Let me have this!

"What now?" Richie moaned.

Ash had been so wrapped up in her own thoughts she hadn't realized they had made it back to the intersection just before Dottie's gas station. A couple of concrete barriers had been put up along the road and behind them a couple of police cars and a pristine fire truck. A younger officer, his uniform pressed, but with sweat staining the pits dark, waved at them from where he kept court on the shoulder.

The car slowed to a stop and Richie leaned out the window. "What the hell, man?"

Would it be grand theft auto if Richie was arrested and she drove his car to civilization? Something to ask at the police station if Richie ended up a guest of the taxpayers.

The officer strolled over to them, but rather than come directly to the window, he moved around to the back of the car first. Ash watched in the side mirror as he angled his head to read their tags. He looked over the top of the car and gave a stiff nod. Shifting her eyes to the front, Ash saw another officer lift up one of those standard issue walkie talkies and speak into it. It would be just her luck if Richie had a warrant out for something.

She knew he had a history of B&E and a couple of misdemeanors, so it wouldn't surprise her.

She really needed to do some self-reflecting.

The officer finally made his way to the driver side window, stepping back rather than leaning in. "Sorry to have to tell you this, kids," he said in a tone that did not at all suggest he was around their age, "but we have some powerlines down across the road just yonder." He lifted his hand and motioned vaguely toward the road running beyond the gas station. The power lines could have been down going back toward I-22 or further South for all the help that wave offered. "It'll be cleared up in a few hours. I know it's inconvenient, but you'll have to head on back to town."

"Are you fucking serious? What is this? A way to keep people at your Podunk town for a shit movie?"

Old Ash would have tried to keep Richie from getting himself in trouble. Newly improved Ash was going to revel in the schadenfreude of watching Richie get his ass handed to him one way or another.

The officer's face turned red, but he plastered on a grin that was less friendly and more please-give-me-a-reason. "Well, I guess it does the trick. But doesn't change the fact you can't get through."

"Are you shitting me?!"

"Not at all," the guy said, still smiling his murderous smile. "They got a crew out now, but all this heat is giving them trouble. Like I said, you head on back and they'll take care of you. Revelation is nothing if not hospitable." He tipped an imaginary hat at them and moseyed—wow, people really did mosey—back to his spot on the shoulder, blocking the way so cars couldn't make their way round in the grass.

Richie slammed the steering wheel before whipping it round, sending his car in a donut that almost certainly left tire marks on the pavement and definitely had Ash's shoulder slamming into the door. "For fuck's sake, Richie!"

He ignored her, choosing instead to peel out, back down toward Revelation. As they were jostled and jolted, they passed a bright blue, minivan on its way out to the main road. Ash could see several car seats. Against one window, a child lay with his or her head cushioned by a blanket, probably worn out from the heat of the day.

Ash turned round in her seat, watching the van disappear around the corner, everything in her screaming to follow, even if she knew they were stuck. She didn't want to go back to Revelation. She didn't want to get any closer to the thing in the woods she may or may not have imagined.

The cicadas buzzed outside, the sound too much like laughter.

CHAPTER TEN

Ash leaned against the dusty car, arms wrapped around herself, unusually cold. After they'd returned to the parking lot, Richie had stormed off somewhere. It had taken all she had to climb back out of the car, the woods in view, but the too-hot leather seats and the stale air finally drove her back onto the asphalt.

With little else to do, Ash picked her way across the lot toward the tents, people still milling around, though not as many as before. All the while, she kept the forest in her periphery. The incident with the husk felt far more dreamlike in the bright sunlight after a routine, midday feud with Richie, but she couldn't shake the feeling something was very wrong, and she truly hoped they would not be stuck in the town overnight.

Not that she'd seen any motel signs.

She snaked through the people and around booths. There had to be some place she could buy overpriced water to clear the dust from her throat. There were less people now, some likely driven into the movie theatre for one of the screenings or onto a trail walk by the heat. Just the thought of the trail had her eyes shifting to the open mouth into the woods. What had been cool and inviting before now seemed more like a gaping tunnel of a mouth.

A probiscis.

"I thought you were beating it out of town?"

Cal was beside her, dark curls damp from the sweat across his forehead. She might have swooned if she weren't completely and utterly horrified by what he held in his hand. "What the actual fuck is that?"

"Ice cream," he said confidently, jerking a thumb at the parked ice cream truck behind him, an older gentleman inside slinging pre-packaged popsicles and drumsticks with a Crypt Keeper grin, the tinny music from the truck's speakers almost drowned out by the sound of the cicadas.

Ash pulled a face, staring at the blue monstrosity in Cal's grip. In a warped way, it resembled a foot. What was unmistakably a pink gumball protruded from what was meant to be the big toe like a hard, glossy boil. "In what unholy dimension is that ice cream?"

He twisted the popsicle stick back and forth. "The 80's, I think." Holding eye contact, he popped the smaller toes into his mouth, biting down. She could hear the soft sound of the molded treat give way, like the press of packing peanuts. He held it out to her, chewing. "Want a lick?"

"Of your *foot*?"

He smiled, his teeth and the inside of his mouth already stained blue. "Not into feet?"

"Not in the least!"

"Good to know," he teased, chomping off the digit holding the gumball. His cheek puffed out like a chipmunk as he tried to chew, the crack loud as he ground the shiny ball between his molars. "Oh yea. Tastes like chalk and cold medicine. Just like childhood."

She laughed and gagged at the same time. "So gross."

"Are we really going to start judging taste here?" he teased, chewing steadily on the gumball while what remained of the foot bled blue dye into the dirt.

She pursed her lips, narrowing her eyes behind her sunglasses.

Cal gave a little chuckle, blowing a bubble which he then popped with his tongue before he went back to smacking it loudly. "Seriously, your boyfriend seems like a douche."

She swiped at the strands of hair floating into her face. "Ex-boyfriend."

"He know that?"

"Not yet. Kind of hard to tell someone to fuck off when you're stranded about a hundred odd miles from anywhere you might be able to get a ticket home."

He tipped his decimated foot toward her, the pale wooden stick poking from the top like a shard of bone. "Touché. You're. . . okay though, right?"

"What do you mean?"

He blushed, his blue stained mouth turning purple. "I mean, you were running like someone was chasing you. And your not-quite-ex-boyfriend doesn't seem like the warmest sort."

If it wasn't such a serious topic and he wasn't trying

to be so nice, she might have laughed. "No, I'm fine. He's just a mouth that I will be getting rid of at the first sign of a Starbucks."

Cal shrugged, finishing off the last of his ice cream. "I'll drive you."

She stepped back in surprise, but he must have taken it for something else because he blushed again, this time darker than before. "Oh, shit. Sorry. That came off very creepy, didn't it?"

She didn't even get a chance to answer when a voice summoned them. "Have y'all gotten your cameras yet?"

They both turned to see a mousy man with Coke bottle glasses and a 70's porn mustache holding a huge duffle bag.

This looked more like someone she would be terrified of.

"Your cameras," he repeated. He unzipped the top of the duffle and hoisted out two small, handheld video recorders, plastic casings scratched. Both were the old school, compact style with the tiny flip screen, rotating viewfinder, and shoulder strap. Ash remembered her dad having one when she was growing up. Glasses man held them out like an offering. "For the movie?"

"The movie?" Ash turned her head to look down the street where the marquis was clearly visible. "*CICADA*? You hand out old camcorders as swag?"

The man had a tittering laugh. "Bless your heart, no. It is more like a game. Everybody gets to pretend they are part of the film. Sort of makes the whole thing a little more fun."

"Oh, like LARPing?" Cal said.

Ash pulled a face. "What the hell is LARPing?"

"Live action role play?"

"Oh my God." Cal was a nerd. A hot nerd with a foot fetish. She could pick 'em.

"Yes!" the man said, nodding so hard his glasses wobbled on his nose. "Just like that! And it is all in fun. Let's you see Revelation in a new way. Let's you be the star of your own movie. The original film was shot on little more than these almost twenty years ago. Isn't that amazing?" He all but shoved them into their hands. "Head on into the movie and get a seat before they're all gone." Before they could argue or ask any more questions, he was off, his duffle bag smacking heavily against his hip. They watched him approach another obvious tourist, someone still trying to find a signal on his phone.

"Well, how about it?"

Ash turned to Cal, his camera trained on her. "What are you doing?"

"Oh, come on," he grinned, watching the little monitor. "It is so hokey you almost have to do it. Just for the experience. Nobody is going to believe this place. Let's go see the movie. Rumor is the road is closed."

"You want to go watch a low budget horror movie with a random stranger?"

He wagged a finger. "Ah, ah! A random bitchy stranger. I have my standards."

"Why are you so weird?"

"I'm into saving people. And saving a cute girl from boredom and her lame, not-quite boyfriend, is noble." He grinned, teeth blue. "Besides, might as well if we're stuck here."

It was not a date, she told herself. It was not. But it was something. Something that might be fun.

"Well, I guess we—"

A terrified scream erupted from the edge of the park.

CHAPTER ELEVEN

The crowd in the park didn't quiet all at once, even while the screams continued, but slowly faded to a dull murmur, oglers craning their necks to see what was happening.

A teenage girl—maybe twenty, but certainly not old enough to drink—stumbled backward till her shoulder clipped the edge of the ice cream trunk, knocking hard enough to disrupt her screams momentarily. A uniformed officer and a woman with a box dyed bob haircut hurried to her side, the woman speaking in soothing tones while the girl just pointed toward a line of blue port-a-potties on the perimeter of the park.

"There! There! In the bushes!"

Morbidly curious and a little desperate to prove she was right before about the thing in the woods, Ash drew closer.

"What, hon?" the lady with the bob asked, petting the girl's hair like she was stroking a cat. "You see a snake, sweetheart? They're everywhere down here."

"*A body!*"

That got the crowd quiet enough.

Before there could be a surge of the nosy busybodies, like Ash had every intention of being, several other officers in uniform rushed forward, including the man who had been directing traffic. He was obviously the one in charge, probably the Sheriff, murmuring directions and pointing fingers so the other cops spread out, keeping the onlookers back.

He approached the girl, still shaking. "Now calm down, miss. Where did you say you saw a body?"

Ash strained to hear as the girl pointed again, indicating the heavy bushes behind the portable toilets. "There! I was in the bathroom, and I heard this weird sound from behind the wall. I don't know what it was, but I thought I heard someone choking! I came out and looked and someone is—" She burst into tears.

Box dye job pulled the girl into a hug, darting a nervous look at the Sheriff.

The Sheriff's face revealed nothing, those aviators concealing his eyes. But he put his hand on his gun and slowly turned, throwing his other hand out. "You boys keep 'em all back."

He unclipped his weapon, but didn't draw, slowly approaching the toilets, one foot crossing over the other. Rather than looking at the ground, his head kept tilting up like he was scanning the sky for something. Finally, he reached the bushes, pushed branches aside, and leaned down.

There was a long silence.

The Sheriff straightened and gave a strange grin. "Well, miss, I see why you were so scared. And it *is* a body. But—" Reaching down with both hands, he pulled something shrunken and misshapen from the brush. It looked like a mummified corpse wearing clothes too big for its frame. One of its shoes—a blue sneaker—tumbled into the bushes as the officer hoisted it up with a bit of a struggle, its limbs like a ragdoll's. The face was hideous, hollowed out and shrunken in.

"Halloween prop, miss, or for the movie, if you will. We have a spooky trail in October, but we drag some of these fellas out for the guided tours. Gives it a bit of ambiance. Kind of like that movie ride at Universal. Somebody was probably hauling some to the trails and this poor fella got jostled off." The cop attempted to wave the skeletal form's arm, but it kept slipping in his grip.

"There now," said the woman, gripping the young girl's shoulders. "That's better. Just a movie prop. And mercy, they do look a fright don't they? I won't go on that haunted trail myself, but the kids certainly love it in the fall." She guided the girl away and round the ice cream truck. "Let's get you something. My treat. And then we'll find you some shade. That had to be *terrifying*! I even have the jitters now!"

But the woman's voice had an edge; a saccharine sweetness to it, certainly, but underneath that something else. Like, she really was a little afraid.

"Bobby?" the Sheriff called, moving into the brush, obscuring their view of the horror doll, "C'mere a second son."

The other young officer hurried over and the two men put their heads together, speaking low. After a quick word, the sheriff slipped quietly into the trees and the other officer hurried out of the park. The shoe that had fallen from the mannequin lay under a fern, half in shadow, abandoned. The officer had obviously forgotten it.

"So, movie?" Cal asked beside her, popping the lens cap onto his camera. "It's cool if not. I just thought—"

"No," Ash said, trying to smile as she forced herself to turn away from the trees and the shoe, desperately attempting to ignore another one of those fiddly feelings like she should be remembering something. "Let's go. I've had enough of baking in this heat for a while. Think it's frying my brain."

Cal remained silent.

"This is where you say it isn't," she encouraged.

He wrinkled his face. "Well. . ."

She held up a finger to his lips. "Shhh. Just. . . be pretty."

He gave her that lopsided grin, lips moving against her finger. "Now if *I* had said something like that—"

"I would have slapped you shitless," she preened, walking away, maybe—okay, definitely!—putting a sway in her hips. It was nice to feel attractive and wanted, instead of like a placeholder for whatever gum-popping infant Richie was likely attempting to court with such romantic poetry as, "U up?"

As Cal caught up to her, he asked, "So, why is everybody stuck in town? I heard other people talking about it, too."

"Some power lines went down and are crossing the highway or something? I don't really know. Richie was being a dick, and I was too annoyed to really pay attention. They just turned us back. But they didn't seem to be rushing, if you know what I mean."

"I don't think they rush here. They mosey."

"What exactly is a mosey?"

Cal shrugged. "I think you know it when you see it."

She laughed and it felt good, like maybe things weren't so bad. Like, maybe she was just being silly and cranky. Not crazy. Cranky. That's it.

As they wove through the park towards main street and the movie theatre, a man with a trim beard and athletic shorts brushed by her, calling for someone. "Todd? Todd?"

Ash turned her head to see the man duck into a tent, thinking he looked familiar. Which is when that pesky feeling from before finally clicked into place. He was one of the men she'd passed on the trail when she'd been running full speed out of the woods. He'd been with another man. A man wearing blue Nikes and a blue shirt, just like the prop body.

CHAPTER TWELVE

The theatre was old; a monument devoted to the nostalgia of a time long past. Pillars. crown molding. and old bannisters all with flaking gold filigree. The air hung heavy with the odor of sweat, popcorn, and fake butter. But underneath, an older smell of must and damp seemed to linger. The faded, patterned carpet was spotted with holes and bare patches exposing the floorboards beneath. How many years of feet and spills had such a place seen?

With only one theatre and one movie showing on a loop, she and Cal flowed in with the crowd. Teenagers dressed in old usher costumes with red vests and faded gold buttons handed them red and white striped cartons of popcorn as they passed, smiling broadly and telling them to enjoy the movie.

Everybody smiled in Revelation. Even the teenagers. It was gross. Or maybe Ash was just cynical. Probably both, but it was still gross.

She and Cal found seats at the end of a row toward the back of the darkened theatre. The dank smell was more evident there, likely from the heavy curtains framing the scratched and marked up screen. Above, the whirring click of the projector put her in mind of the cicadas outside. There was apparently no escaping the noise.

Ash didn't want to think about the abandoned shoe. Didn't want to think about the gentleman searching for Todd. And she certainly didn't want to think about that horrible, ghoulish prop. And since it was either that or a cheesy horror film with a hottie who'd stroked her ego, she chose the latter.

They'd missed the opening, so they spent the first few minutes squinting at the grainy images on the screen, trying to decipher what was happening. It certainly looked like an early found footage film. Very low budget and rather terrible cinematography. It reminded her of *The Blair Witch Project* in a lot of ways, but the cast seemed bigger and there didn't seem to be a greater plot. As far as she could tell, it was just a bunch of people with cameras moving around the town. Hey, Sally's! was there. So was the laundromat and the gazebo in the park, paint fresh. It was kind of funny to think she'd spent the day on a movie set.

"Do you know what's happening?" she whispered.

Cal leaned closer, breath smelling of popcorn. "I'm a little lost, but I think it is this family on vacation? I don't recognize any of the actors."

How could you? The quality was home movie, which she supposed had been the aesthetic the director was shooting for. Everything took on a sepia tint and the angles tilted so dramatically at times, it made Ash's stomach flip.

There was a long shot of the dad holding the camera in front of a store window so he could wave at his reflection. Ash could see the camera, the same style slung over her arm and wedged up against the chair. It was clever marketing, she thought, if a little limiting. If you wanted something to seem authentic, you only released it in the style it had been filmed. You certainly wouldn't earn much from the production, but maybe it was more about the art. It had to have been for the director and writer of *CICADA*. Already half an hour into the film and there was little happening beyond weird cuts of a family vacationing in the middle of nowhere during some kind of town fair. And through it all, that faint background buzz of the cicadas in the trees.

Ah, she thought. The broader connection. The film took place during Revelation's own cicada festival and that had later been influenced by the movie. The director and writer were probably locals who had cast their own families or friends. No way were the actors not related. The two bored looking teenagers in the movie looked like carbon-copies of their on-screen parents.

She chewed almost mechanically on her popcorn and settled a bit deeper into the seat, enjoying the squeak of hinges and how the well-worn plush cradled her, trying to fall into the film.

On screen, the family decided to go for a walk in the woods, the foursome walking a trail as the mom tried to point out things that were "pretty" or "interesting" in hopes of engaging the children she so obviously wanted to reconnect with. The boy would offer monosyllabic responses the mother tried to pretend were encouraging.

The teenage girl had nothing but attitude, complaining that everything and anything was stupid, and they could have had a real vacation at the beach like all her friends instead of the lamest road trip ever. The girl was probably going to lose both parents and have to fight the giant monster off while covered in red corn syrup. There would be a lot of jostling camera footage as she ran through the woods in the dark, crashing through underbrush and panting erratically.

It was all such a predictable formula Ash considered nodding off, finding herself comfortable and cool and not sharing breathable air with a fucktwit boyfriend. She could just shut her eyes and tell Cal to wake her when it was over.

But instead, the next shot had her sitting up so quickly she knocked the remaining popcorn from her lap and onto the floor.

The room erupted in whoops and claps. Ash ignored them all as she focused on the screen, her hands clutching the armrests tight. The camera zoomed in and out on a huge growth on a tree. The actors were speculating as to what it was: a carving, a totem, a weird tree tumor. The 'dad' got closer, zooming in on the bulbous growth that looked eerily like a head.

The theatre went silent.

Ash tried to brace herself, reminded herself it was a damn horror movie, and a jump scare was inevitable. But she wasn't watching the film. She was back in the woods, stumbling into a conifer grove and finding a growth on a tree. Getting closer. Closer.

On screen, something rustled inside the lump, and

Ash lurched back in her seat while the audience roared. The actor screamed and stumbled back, the camera jerking wildly, a wild swirl of ground, treetops, and sky as he righted himself, panting for breath.

Ash was up and moving down the aisle and out through the lobby. Not looking where she was going, she slammed into one of the usherettes and only mumbled something that might have been an apology or just something cruel, head spinning. She couldn't think till she was back outside on the sidewalk, under the marquis in the heat, skin cold and clammy, trying to suck in deep breaths of hot, humid air.

"Hey," Cal said, coming up beside her, carrying her abandoned bag and camera. "You okay? You could have said you didn't like horror movies."

"That's what I saw."

"Huh?"

Men! She snatched her bag a little forcefully and whipped her phone out, rapidly tapping the screen till she found the picture she'd taken in the forest and turned it to face Cal. "This! The thing in the woods!"

"Oh yeah. You're right. It does look the same. You must have stumbled onto the old movie set. You even said it moved, right? It must be something they have in the woods to scare tourists. That's kind of cool, actually."

"What?" Did he hear himself? "No. This place is weird. It's all just weird!"

Cal clicked his tongue. "Let's go ask."

What? "What?"

"Come on."

He wasn't saying she was crazy, he was trying to offer

explanations, rationale. It set her teeth on edge. As if someone couldn't be both reasonable and emotional at the same time.

But fine. She'd see where this was going. Not like she had anything better to do.

* * *

The video store was like the indie video rental place they'd had down the street from her house growing up. Not the painted, bright yellow walls of a Blockbuster, but with dark, wood paneled walls, shit lighting, and hand-written signs for each genre. The shelves were just particle board and the whole room felt sort of dirty and gloomy.

All of that would have been one thing, but the only thing on the shelves were VHS tapes. No DVDs or Blu-rays or even the forgotten HD DVDs. Only VHS. The book-sized box sleeves were all worn, the covers sun-faded. On one wall she saw a huge collection of the old plastic Disney VHS tapes. The same kind she'd had at her parents' house growing up. Wild.

And on TVs mounted in each corner, that fucking *CICADA* movie was playing.

What she wouldn't give for a baseball bat.

"Can I help you?" A man with a paunch stomach and oily hair wearing a screen printed *CICADA* T-shirt stood behind an old wooden counter, movie posters tacked along the front. *JAWS. PLATOON. TITANIC. THE GRADUATE.*

"Hey," Cal said cheerfully, walking to the desk.

"Wow. This place takes me back to when I was a little kid."

The man puffed up proudly. "That's what we like to hear. We like to take you back to a more innocent time."

Cal whistled, head pivoting. "I mean, this is really something."

"Well, thank you," the man chuckled, swiping a hand across the old wood of the desk. "Always nice when visitors appreciate it. Now I know y'all aren't here for a rental, obviously, but I've got plenty of CICADA merch at the ready." He gestured to the pegboard wall behind him where screen printed T-shirts, embroidered hats, and other cheesy items were on display. A cicada Christmas ornament? No fucking way.

Pulling his wallet from his back pocket, Cal pointed with his free hand. "Can I get a hat, actually?"

"Sure!" The man pulled down a red trucker hat embroidered with twisty, vine like writing that read CICADA. "That'll be fifteen."

"Not bad prices around here, either," Cal complimented, passing cash over as he shoved the hat on his head. "A hat like this might be forty dollars anywhere else."

Ash milled around the racks of tapes, lifting a few just to make sure they weren't props. The whole town felt too weird to be real and she no longer would have been surprised to find it all to be a movie set.

"Not in Revelation. We try to keep things simple and fair," the man said, shaking his head. "Especially during cicada season. We want y'all to feel well treated when you're here for such a short time."

Ash had to ask just out of curiosity. "What's with all the VHS tapes?"

"It's the way we do things. Sometimes the old ways are the best ways," the man said with a light in his eyes Ash didn't find creepy at all.

Ok, a little. Weird, cryptic fucker.

Cal cleared his throat awkwardly. "Wonder if you could give us some info. We saw this in the woods and we're wondering what it is."

Ash had to give Cal credit for not leading the witness. She held her phone out, showing the photo. The man's mouth stretched into a smile that didn't quite make it past cringe. "Oh. That. Haven't y'all seen the movie?"

"No," Ash blurted.

"Oh, you should! There is one in the movie. Of those, I mean. It sort of kicks it off."

"Right. That makes sense," Cal said, voice full of saccharine laced sarcasm. "So, they're what? Carvings?"

"Oh. Uh. Yeah. Just sort of movie props," the man stuttered.

"And they don't have like motors or anything?" She jerked a thumb at Cal with a giggle. "My friend thought he saw it move and I told him it was just the heat."

She ignored the amused look Cal shot her. "Haha. No. No," the clerk said, tapping his hands across the desk. "That heat'll mess with you. Would you excuse me a second?"

"Sure! We'll just be headed out," Cal said, but the guy was already headed to the back of the store, passing under one of the television sets and through a curtain of beads that clacked as he went. There was the metallic *thunk* of a door being opened and sharp, hurried footsteps.

Ash tiptoed to the back, leaning around the corner near a shelf of old black and white films so she could peek at the wizard behind the curtain.

She couldn't see much. Not without stepping out and being seen, but she could see a high shelf and boxes, the kind people used for files. They were labeled in black Sharpie. *CICADA '89. CICADA '06. CICADA UNCUT.* Sequels and extra footage? Was this squirrely dude the director?

There was a hiss of static and a whispered voice from somewhere behind the door and Ash tensed, waiting. "This is Will. Someone on the council, pick up. Over." A digital beep.

Then another. "What's going on, Will? Over." Ash recognized the voice. The lady from the parking lot. Annaliese.

Will's voice dropped so quiet Ash could only hear every couple of words. "Someone saw. . . waking up. . . too early. . ."

The beeps ending and beginning. "Roger, Will. We'll get eyes out. Over."

What the fuck was going on in Revelation?

CHAPTER THIRTEEN

Back out on the street, Cal kept his hands in his pockets, eyes shaded under the brim of his new hat, contemplative. Ash tried not to look around, feeling watched.

"You believe me? About what I heard?" She had to know if Cal was an ally or just someone else who thought she was crazy.

"Yeah," he said without hesitation. "I just don't know what to think about it. I keep coming up with thoughts. That it's all for this movie with some kind of big reveal before it gets too dark." But he didn't sound as sure as he had earlier.

Somehow that made her feel a little better. Misery did love company.

"I just want to leave. I don't care about the road-blocks or the stupid film reenactments or dumb fireworks."

Cal halted. "Fireworks?"

"Yeah. The parking attendant told me there were fireworks tonight in the park. The cops mentioned it, too."

"They can't shoot off fireworks there. That conifer

forest is pure kindling right now. And this place is a funnel. Why not just light the town on fire and save time. Listen," he said, voice with a sudden edge. "I've got to go find their fire marshal. But offer stands. You want a ride to the next exit or the next, fine by me. I'm the red Ford Ranger at the far end of the lot. But if you take your chances with slick, no hard feelings." He held out his hand with a lopsided grin, "It was nice to feet you either way."

"Oh my God, you're such a nerd," she said with a snort. "No promises, but if you come back with one of those disgusting foot ice creams again, I will absolutely know you are an ax murderer and then it is an automatic NOPE."

After they parted ways, she returned to the lot and checked for Cal's truck. Just in case. 'Cause maybe. What did she have to lose? Her life if he turned out to be a serial killer? Pssh. She was at risk of losing that to the justice system if she remained on the road with Richie any longer.

A blurred shape flew past her face and landed on the roof of Richie's car. Or sort of landed. A bug had fallen onto its back and was spinning in mad circles, trying to get upright, buzzing like mad. She recognized it immediately. A cicada, its belly bright white, little legs kicking and thrashing, wings caught beneath. It spun so out of control it rolled right off the back of the roof, bouncing off the trunk and onto the ground.

Ash rounded the back wheel and stooped to get a closer look, leaning over the creature, shoving her glasses up onto her head. The bug was upright now and unmoving in the shadow she cast. Maybe it was stunned. Its red eyes looked like perfectly round berries glued to its matte black head and its golden veined wings crackled like paper.

It looked harmless enough.

But she still remembered that thing in the trees and she eased back on her heels. As she did, the bug gave a rattle and crack and flew off so suddenly, zipping away into the sunshine, Ash gave a little squeal and plopped backwards onto her butt.

"Great. Spooked by everything. And now I'm talking to myself again." She got ready to stand when she noticed the back of Richie's car. Low on the license plate, opposite the registration decal, was a round sticker. The kind you might find slapped onto STOP signs or crosswalks by kids promoting local bands. But this one was the same she'd seen in the diner on all the license plates on the wall, the little green cicada waving an arm in greeting or farewell.

Why would someone tag Richie's car with a stupid sticker?

She stood, dusting the seat of her shorts off, an idea occurring to her. She started drifting through the lot, casually glancing at plates. Some had stickers. Some did not. Most of the cars with the stickers were small sedans or some pickup trucks, which made her think of something else.

Ash looked up and down the lot, shielding her eyes, searching. But the van wasn't there. The one they had passed on the road with the kid asleep. It had hit the roadblock only a couple of minutes after them. It would have been turned back. So why wasn't it here? In fact, more spaces were empty than filled. The lot had been packed before.

Her skin prickled. The movie. The video store. Now this?

The Sherriff who'd carted off the dummy was back to directing traffic, wiping his forehead with a red handkerchief. At Ash's approach, he grinned. "Enjoyin' the fun?"

"Sure," she said absently. "Um. . . Could you tell me if the roadblock is gone? If they fixed the power lines so we can, ya know, get out of dodge?" She hoped that if maybe she spoke the lingo she might get a better response.

"Oh, I don't think so. They said it would take some time. Don't worry, though! Still plenty left to happen!" He smiled, broad and toothy.

She matched his shit-eating grin with her own, batting her lashes behind her pink glasses. "Could you check for me? I'm sorry to put you out. I just know we really need to be getting on the road."

His smile didn't waver, but his throat bobbed a bit. He unclipped his walkie from his belt and pressed the flat black button on the side. She really, really hoped he wasn't on the same channel as video store Willy. "Hey, Pauly, you there, son?"

A crackle of static and then a disembodied voice from the walkie. "Yes, sir."

"That mess with the *lines*," the officer drawled, drawing the 'I' out so long Ash could see down his pink throat. "They don't happen to have that cleaned up, right?"

There was a long silence and then Pauly responded. "Oh no. It's goin' be awhile yet. You got trouble?"

"No, not at all! Just a lovely young thing wanting to check how things were proceeding. I know you boys are doing your best."

Both his tone and his smile made her want to smash his teeth in with the butt of his gun. She made sure she smiled wider, turning her face into a grimace as she thanked him for absolutely nothing. Back in the shade of the laundromat, she leaned her head against the cool bricks, the rough edges catching strands of her hair, wondering if there was somewhere she could get a decent iced coffee.

"Did you get anywhere with Sheriff Buford?"

The pretty girl with the dreads had joined her on the corner, dark skin dewy and radiant while Ash was sure she looked a complete hot mess in comparison.

"Sorry?"

"Buford? Smokey and the Bandit?" At Ash's clearly vacant expression, the girl shrugged. "Doesn't matter. Did the local law enforcement give any indication as to when we will be released?"

"Oh! No, but not to worry," Ash said, lowering her voice and putting a twang into her words. "The boys are doing their best to fix the liiiiiiiiiiiiines so the pretty things don't need to worry none." She fake spat onto the sidewalk and tugged her shorts up by the belt loops.

The girl's lips turned up in a smile. "They've gotten to you. Soon, you'll be one of them."

The fuck they would, Ash vowed silently. But this felt

like an opening. "Hey. I don't want to sound, you know," she would not say crazy, "but—"

"Is this place fucking weird?"

Ash sagged in relief. "Yes!"

"This place is fucking *Twilight Zone* and I hate it." She stuck out her hand. "I'm Charlie."

"Ash."

Charlie tossed her dreads, the colors swirling round her head, shielding her eyes from the steadily lowering sun and glowered at the park. Along her forearm, Ash saw a thin line of a tattoo. An ombre rainbow not much wider than a piece of string. It was pretty. "I don't know. I'm starting to think this is a bunch of bullshit."

A kindred spirit at last! "Thank you! It doesn't make sense, right?"

"Nope. I've been going steadily round this state park for days. Stopping in every little town and nobody ever mentioned this place or this festival to me. Not once. But I stopped at some gas station and now I've been here all day. All day. I hear about their plan for fireworks, and I make a bit of noise because, wow, how irresponsible, and now I can't even leave? At first, I thought they were just punishing me for that and asking if they had vegan options around town."

"You monster."

"Yeah. But don't you notice how thinned out it has gotten? There are still plenty of people, but not as many as there should be if the road is closed." Charlie leaned closer, the beads in her hair clicking. "I've been watching, and some cars have not come back. But you just asked Andy Griffith and he said it is still closed. Doesn't make sense."

"And what is with this movie and that whole LARPing business?"

"What is LARPing?"

"Live action role play, and I just learned that was a thing today. But the cameras? Look." She pointed to a couple of college-aged boys wearing horror T-shirts on the edge of the tree line. One was filming while another pretended to see something in the forest. He was taking a few steps into the trees, slowly, putting on. "Something about that movie they are showing."

"Ohhhhh, some dude tried to hand me one of those camera things and I declined. Those tapes don't decompose for a thousand years and are full of toxins." When she saw Ash push hers a little behind her hip she just laughed. "Don't worry. I'm not shaming you. My opinion never has to be anybody else's. That would make me a bitch."

Ash grinned. "Oh, I'm absolutely a bitch, but not for those reasons."

"Fair enough."

The guy taping his friend crept closer to the trees, calling for his buddy. "I do agree with you, though," Ash said. "All day I've been weirded out, and it just keeps getting weirder."

Her eyes caught quick movement along the edge of the trees where the two guys had been moments before. Both were gone.

On the ground, dropped onto a patch of grass, was

one of the video cameras, its lens a black eye staring back at Ash.

CHAPTER FOURTEEN

"Uh..."

Okay, so it wasn't profound, but Ash's brain was obviously scrambled from the heat and annoyance and therefore she was unable to articulate properly what she had clearly meant to say. Something along the lines of, *I'm beginning to think we're fucked.*

There was something menacing about the abandoned camera, its unblinking eye pointed in their direction and the unnatural movement just before. It had been too fast. The guy had been standing there, calling his friend, and then a blur of motion. That's all she'd caught out of the corner of her eye.

Charlie followed her stare. "Where'd those two clowns go?"

Ash had no answer, just a sickening feeling of dread as she continued to hold a staring contest with the recorder.

"Attention, ladies and gentlemen," came a booming voice over some sort of sound system. Charlie and Ash both winced at the deafening volume. "If you would please make your way to the center of town toward the gazebo. For you *CICADA* movie fans, we are going to have a few surprises. Sorry for the short notice, but we wouldn't want you to miss this! Afterwards, there will be a general announcement about the road conditions. We know some of y'all are with us accidentally, but we do hope we've made your stay special. Having you here is such a blessing."

People who had been milling from one place to the next began to head toward the park. The officer Ash had spoken to was waving people down the road. Behind him on the opposite side of the street, the parking attendant and the guy with the cameras were hurrying down toward the residential road. They kept looking up, like they were watching for something, Annaliese's dangling earrings catching the sun's fading rays.

She spotted Cal and she called out to him. He turned at her voice and reversed directions, coming to stand with her and Charlie. "Their fire department is a joke. My 'concerns,'" he said making air quotes with his fingers, "were noted and would be passed down." He shook his head and noticed Charlie. "Hey."

"Hey," she said blandly.

Ash was no longer watching the lines of movie lovers and detoured tourists, but the shop windows along Main Street. Lights inside went dark and CLOSED signs started appearing on doors. A reasonable person might think all the owners were shutting down early to head to the festival's finale.

And yet. . .

Charlie groaned and pushed off the wall like she meant to follow the herd, but Ash put out a hand. "No."

"What?"

"I don't know. I just don't want to go." That felt safe and not crazy.

"Works for me. I'm over this crap anyway. Come on." Charlie grabbed her hand and tugged her along the wall.

"Where are we going?" Ash asked, Cal following behind.

"Let's just hang out here." They slipped behind the building, the woods on their left, but a clear view of the park and the masses among the tents.

And Richie storming towards them.

"Where have you been all day?"

She ignored him, leaning to see over his shoulder. The crowd was getting restless. Plenty had their VHS recorders out, ready to capture bonus footage for their tribute film. What she didn't see was a local. Not one. Porn-stache man and Annaliese were gone. But she didn't see the old man or Amy or whoever from the restaurant. Even the cops were gone.

Her eyes drifted again to the abandoned recorder.

"Hey, Richie? Will you grab that real quick?" she asked, pointing to the recorder.

"Why?"

Because I don't want to get any closer to those trees. Maybe it made her horrible, but she was okay with that considering. "Just please."

He gave her the stink eye, but scooped it up and trudged back, twisting it round before passing it to her. "Still on."

Ash stopped the recording and flipped open the screen, pressing down on the rewind button. There was a click and a whir as the tape wound back. Static shot across the screen, blurring the footage as it played too fast for her eyes to track in reverse. Finally, figuring she'd gone back far enough, she hit the little square to stop the tape, feeling the thud inside the machine as the wheels halted. She hit play. The volume was down.

One guy looking into the camera as his friend filmed. He fixed his hair, probably feeling silly. The camera wobbled a little, the operator likely used to a cell phone instead of a two-pound plastic brick. On screen, the friend made a goofy face and then jumped, head snapping to the trees.

The camera turned to the woods, but Ash didn't see anything. The guy on screen inched closer, head moving around like he was trying to catch sight of something as he took a few steps into the forest. The camera angle changed again, toward Charlie and Ash, zooming in on their asses.

Charlie made a sound of disgust. "Why are men?"

The camera jerked round suddenly. But he'd not zoomed back out, so the view was distorted, the camera unable to focus. Trunks of trees, branches, grass: a kaleidoscope of greens and browns. As the images danced, Ash finally found the volume dial with her thumb, feeling it release as she rolled it up. At first, all she could hear was the cicadas buzzing. Or was it static? Louder and louder till it was almost a roar and then a hiss. The camera operator let out a strangled sound she could barely hear over those stupid bugs before the camera went tumbling, falling to the ground with a crack and clatter. On screen, she and Charlie turned at the sound.

She pressed the stop button with a loud *click*.

It was oddly silent.

Which was wrong. All day the cicadas had rattled in her brain like the worst possible case of tinnitus, but no longer. It was, as they said so often in movies, too quiet.

"Uh," Charlie said, echoing Ash's earlier sentiment.

And then the screams began.

CHAPTER FIFTEEN

There was some advice someone had told Ash once when she was younger and going to her first big concert. If some asshole tried anything, she shouldn't yell for help, but instead start screaming, "FIRE!" Something about lizard brains and the way people prioritized their own safety needs.

The screams only a hundred yards or so away in the park drew the small group's attention, but none of them moved. There was something about the primal quality of the screams impossibly mixed with. . . laughter? The tents blocked most of the view, but Ash could see some people backing away or outright running while others stood laughing, cameras poised (some with their phones recording while others held those silly VHS things). Ash couldn't see what they were looking at, but she could hear another noise. A hoarse, deep throated hum.

The screams took on a fever pitch. More people began running, colliding into tent poles or each other, crashing to the ground. Some fled to the street or ran for their cars. And all the while, Ash and the others stood behind the laundromat, watching the chaos unfold. Ash felt somehow separated from whatever was happening, like she was watching it on a screen.

And that was finally what broke the spell.

"Guys. . ."

But the word was drowned out by horns and the roar of engines. There was no hope of getting to the cars, the lot jammed with people trying to leave, only to find themselves smashing bumpers and scraping paint. Everybody was running. But from what?

"Let's get inside," Cal said, ushering them to the backdoor of the laundromat. Gripping the knob in his hand, he grunted. "Locked."

Richie shoved him out of the way. "Move. I got it." He'd shown Ash in the first weeks of dating how he could pick locks. It should have been a red flag, but if he could get them in, she'd wave that flag like the color guard at a football game.

People ran toward the houses in a long line down main street, climbing porch steps and pounding on doors. Others sprinted toward the front of town, trying to catch up to cars. Even more banged on the front of businesses now shuttered and dark.

It was Charlie who saw it first. "What is that?"

Nobody asked what she was referring to. Self-preservation, deeply coded into their genetic material, had them all locating the danger as soon as one of their little pack sounded the alarm. But none of them likely recognized it. Save for Ash who had seen it before on the tree in the woods and again at the screening of that stupid movie. The thing that had crawled from that hole and moved within its impossible husk. A cicada bigger than any bug had a right to be. She had been right, not crazy.

It was not the time to gloat.

The creature buzzed as it flew over the crowd, its pale abdomen vibrating violently like the tail of a rattlesnake. Its wings caught the golden light of the sun setting behind the tops of the pines. It arched and dove and with each dip it grabbed someone as they tried to get away, moving back and forth so quickly Ash thought at first there might be more than one. But it was just too fast. And there were so many people...

Behind her, Richie slapped the door with his hand. "In!" He twisted the knob and basically fell inside, the rest of them rushing in, Ash at the rear.

"Wait!" a voice called as she tried to shut the door. A man and woman, shirts covered with sweat, and another woman in a purple velour jumpsuit—in this heat?!—older, black, her curls trimmed tight to her head and almost completely grey, all came in a rush. The older woman pumped her arms as she walked quickly, hands in loose fists while the other two stumbled and huffed across the concrete.

"Hurry!" Ash yelled, wanting nothing more than to slam the door shut, but unwilling to be so cruel.

The man was rounding hoods and moving between cars easily, his thin frame letting him squeeze past. His wife or girlfriend was having a harder time. She kept swiping at her eyes, her mascara and eyeliner so heavy they had run and pooled into tar pits. The man hurried in past Ash, almost smashing into the doorframe, followed closely by the elderly woman.

"Shut the door!" someone screamed from inside, but Ash only bounced on her heels, staring at the woman still trying to reach them.

She finally made it to edge of the parking lot and Ash could hear her hoarse, rattling breath. Smoker's lungs. Her shoe caught on the curb and down she went, what little air in her body bursting out of her with a tight squeal. Even then, Ash might have rushed forward to help as she struggled to get her legs under her, but a blurred, black object swept in low over the lot and landed right on her back. Ash and the woman both screamed, as black, hairy legs wrapped around her torso, transparent wings turning the world into a blur behind them. And suddenly, Ash was yanked backward, and Richie flung her across the space, still screaming. With a grunt, Richie swung the heavy door closed and locked it.

"It got her! It got her!" Ash mewled, adrenaline flooding her body.

"Breathe," Cal urged, holding her shoulders. "Breathe. Like before. Breathe."

She replicated his breath again. In. Hold. Out. In. Hold. Out. Slowly, her brain and body began to quiet, Cal's hands holding her together.

They found themselves all crammed together in some sort of backroom, empty clothing racks and stacked boxes of detergents and dry-cleaning supplies along the walls. A long window ran the length of the room near the ceiling. Through it, Ash could see nothing but sky and a shadow crisscrossing what was left of the light.

"What was that?" Richie asked, voice a nasal whine.

"Cicada," the man coughed, voice hoarse. "The Cicada. Real. Holy shit. And it got Kelly."

The old woman wiped her hands on the sleeves of her jumpsuit. "Are we safe here, y'all?" She spoke with a thick Southern accent, head swiveling to take in the small room.

Ash didn't think they'd been safe since they'd crossed into town.

"We need to check the front door," Charlie said.

Cal slowly opened the door leading further in the laundromat and was met by a dark hallway. Everyone gathered close behind him, brushing against each other. They walked past the bathrooms and into the open laundry, the place packed with washers and dryers, the huge commercial kind with slots for quarters. A heavy black machine for change stood next to the front desk which wrapped around in a C-shape. In the middle of the room were heavy tables for folding and hanging racks and a few smaller machines for quick loads. The lights were all on, the buzz of the fluorescents overhead a paltry imitation of the buzz of the creature outside, but the front doors were locked, a steel shuttered gate covering the entire front of the store.

They congregated by the front in the small lobby. The older woman sank into a chair, fingers against her lips. She looked as shaken as Ash felt.

The wiry man scratched at his bearded jaw, his face pale as old milk. "It got Kelly. The Cicada got her. It really did."

"From the movie? Get a grip," Richie coughed, though he was fidgeting and nervous.

The guy ignored him. "There are rumors, you know. Like, all these movies from all over the world of found footage before it was even really a thing, right? And people swear the people aren't actors. They aren't billed or if they are, you can't find anything out about them. Like they weren't real people. Like, crisis actors or something. But if you start looking, you find how some people went missing and you start comparing the pictures, right? Lots of people think these aren't movies, but *real*. And *CICADA* is one of the weirdest, yeah?" He was ranting, gesticulating wildly with his hands, eyes feverish. "You don't really see the thing much. Just little impressions or something. Too many close-ups or not in frame. It's what made it so popular! 'Cause it is so real! And there's lots of people on the boards who swear the family was a real family. A cold case from the early 2000s. There are other rumors that there is even an *older* version and *CICADA* is a reboot! But nobody has a copy or anything. Not that anybody has proven. But it has a following! A hardcore fan base! So when invites went out to some of the biggest fans on the boards for the film festival, it was huge! And fuck trying to resell the tickets! One guy tried and—"

"Wait. Stop," Cal said, shaking his head in disbelief. "You were invited here?"

Enthusiastic nods. "Me and Kelly and a bunch of other fans. But it was a big secret. You weren't supposed to talk on the boards about where you were headed because we were gonna get exclusive info, you know? Like, they wanted NDAs and shit. Cool with me 'cause there was no way Kelly and I would miss it. We live for these movies. Our VHS collections are insane! We—" He stopped, remembering there was no 'we' anymore.

"It really was a trap," Charlie laughed, scratching at her scalp with her nails, rustling her dreads.

"Well, I didn't come here 'cause of some movie," said the older woman, cutting in. "I was doing a little road trip in memory of my husband. We always did like a road trip." She smiled poignantly, spinning her wedding ring on her finger. "I just got lost. Damn GPS went out. I've told my grandson I don't like using that thing. Wait till I see that little shit at Christmas." She patted her cheeks with her hands. "I'm Eileen, by the way."

"I'm Warren," the guy said, voice thick.

"Warren," Cal repeated, putting a hand on his shoulder. "I'm Cal. I'm really sorry about Kelly."

Nose red, eyes glassy, Warren looked like Ash felt. "I'm not sure how to feel. We just sort of met today. Been talking for years on the boards. But finally met in person for the first time. Now she's gone?" He looked around like she might be hiding. "She's gone, right? This isn't one of those stupid reality shows where only a couple of people aren't in on the joke?"

"Looked real enough to me," Eileen said, "even though I was busy hustlin'." Her watch beeped and she tapped at the screen, purple nails painted to match her suit clicking across the plastic. She tsked, muttering about miles and heart rates. "Sorry, y'all. What I was sayin' is I was doin' my walkin'. I'm a power walker. Have been for years since my Terry—that was my husband— passed. Bad heart. I'm not goin' like that. I make sure to get my five miles a day. I was doing a lap when they made all that fuss about gettin' over to the park. I was just roundin' the corner when I heard that sound. It was like a cicada, I'll give you that, but if one had a chainsaw. Then I saw someone just go flyin' up through the air, kickin' and hollerin' and Lord. . ." She put a hand on her heart, watch beeping again. She sniffed, tears appearing in the corners of her eyes as she again fumbled with the settings. "Drat."

Ash wandered over to the front door, the street-facing side of the building entirely made up of windows, the steel gate down on the other side. She pressed her ear to the glass, listening to the sounds of panic outside. Sounds she might have associated with the end of the world in an apocalyptic film.

She pressed back. "Warren? In the movie. How do they kill it?"

CHAPTER SIXTEEN

"Kill it?"

"It's a horror movie," Ash reasoned. "How do they kill the monster in the end?"

Warren shook his head. "They don't. It gets them all. One by one. And others." He lifted a shaking hand back the way they came. "What you saw out there? Yeah. That happened in the movie, too. A crowd and the cicada flies down. I thought it was a gag at first. I really did."

Which explained the laughter. The slow dawning realization people had of real danger. These were film fans. They thought it was all part of the show.

"Wait." Charlie shushed. Popping noises from outside.

"Gunshots," Cal whispered. "The police?"

"Good," Richie said. "Let them kill it."

Ash gave a snort of derision. "Not a chance."

"What's that?" Eileen asked, patting her brow with a lilac handkerchief. "You don't think they can?"

Ash shrugged. "I don't think they will. Look at what happened. They kept us here. Told us all a crap story about some power lines down, but didn't you notice?

Cars left and didn't come back." She thought of the stickers on the tags. That's how they knew who to let go. "They selected us."

"Why would they do that?"

"For that thing," Ash said.

"So," Charlie said, worrying her lip, "you think they're shooting. . ."

No hesitation. "I think that's either suppressing fire or they are shooting at people trying to get away."

Richie rubbed his eyes, his leg dancing like he'd suddenly developed restless leg syndrome. She could hear loose change or his keys bouncing in his pocket. "Ash, Christ. This town is fucking weird, but there isn't like a conspiracy to ritually sacrifice people. God you're so c—"

"Shut up, Richie," Ash said, squaring up, getting right up into his face. "I swear that I will feed you to that thing myself if you call me crazy one more fucking time!"

"The cameras," Warren said, pointing to the recorder hanging forgotten from Ash's shoulder. "That's why they handed them out. We were all helping them make the next in the franchise. Holy shit!" He gripped his thin hair in two fists, pulling.

Ash pulled the camera around, weighing it in her hands. What had Charlie said? The film took thousands of years to decompose or something. Durable, but not high def. The more you copied it, the worse it looked. Anything digital would make it easy to identify faces. But grainy taped footage? The film they watched in that theatre looked like a shitty home movie because, like

Warren said, it *was* a shitty home movie. True found footage.

There was the crash of glass from the back of the laundromat.

Charlie made a soft noise in the back of her throat and Cal raised a finger to his lips. He waved his free hand, gesturing for all of them to hide. There was a flurry of activity, the frantic squeak of sneakers on linoleum as everyone tried to find a hiding spot.

Ash chose an industrial dryer and hopped inside, squeezing herself into the drum, limbs at odd angles in the tight space. She could not shut the top completely. She turned her head sideways on her neck, her ear against the lid, and tried to think small. A faint crack remained, just a slit of light. And though she tried, she could no more close her eyes than she could the lid.

That chainsaw buzz, crashes, and things falling came from the back. Then a skittering sound in the greater room. Something moved just out of her line of sight with the telltale crackling of the cicada.

Suddenly, it leapt into the air to land with a crash onto the center units, its many legs like black tree branches dancing and scraping across the too-white appliances. Ash felt the scream in her chest, heard it in her own ears just below the sound of her blood pounding, but nothing escaped her lips. Nothing could have. She was too terrified to scream.

It was one thing to see the thing outside. Outside it had been almost unbelievable. Given enough time, she could have convinced herself that what she had seen was not nearly as horrifying as she had first imagined. But not up close in those unforgiving lights. It was enough like a regular cicada, but too much like something other. The head too much like. . .

A human head.

No wonder people thought it was someone in an intricately designed costume. The head was deceptive, lending it a greater camouflage. She might have taken it for distressed neoprene; the kind divers wore, molded and artfully sculpted by a master costumer. But no. It was real. Too horrible not to be real. Seeing it under fluorescents, wings folded down its back, twitching and sending tiny prisms of light though its iridescent membranes, its bulbous, humanoid head and bulging eyes, red and wrong and horrible. . . Ash would never close her eyes again without seeing this thing behind her lids.

She was afraid her heart was about to burst from her body as its strange head, alien and bizarre, scanned the room. Long fibrous hairs, rigid and wiry, sprouted from its legs and face. Its body dipped and shuddered, sending short bursts of that rattle, turning the washing machines into steel drums. A cacophony of noise erupted in the room, bouncing off the walls, shaking the lid against Ash's head and she began to pray.

Don't let it find us.

The cicada's many feet danced atop the machines and Ash was reminded of the banner in the square painted with the cartoonish version. It had been so silly. So whimsical. Nothing like this nightmare. An eldritch god ruling over a town of evil monsters.

It scampered off the washers, running on hairy, quick

feet toward the front of the laundry. Ash followed it with her eye, losing it when it moved too far beyond her periphery. There was the sound of something falling to the floor with a bang and then screams. Ash twisted her head ever so slightly. *Oh God.*

Warren was up against the blue painted wall, panicked, spitting breaths between clenched teeth as he kicked out with this work boots as the creature pressed close, holding him fast. There was a sharp click and the sickening sound of something wet and Warren's face lost all color as he stared at the monster. He gave one last pleading sound before what looked to be a long black spike drove straight through his right eye. Warren twitched against the wall, gurgling noises coming from his open mouth. There was an underlying sound, something faint and foreign and strangely familiar. And Warren began to shrink before her eyes, getting smaller. Or thinner, as if the cicada had punched a hole in a Warren balloon with that spike and all the air was draining out. His arms seemed to shrink. His throat hollowed out. His cheekbones jutted so sharply in his face she thought they might pierce through his skin, now hanging loose and baggy.

Drinking from the roots of trees with their straw mouths. Sluuuuuuuuuuuuuurp!

A probiscis.

Danton. The old man had made that sound, wet and almost obscene, telling her how certain insects drained the nectar from plants using a probiscis. But this cicada —this monster—had apparently evolved to require a much richer nutrient.

It was eating Warren. Sucking his internal juices through that hideous black straw. It drank and drank long after Warren stopped twitching, his voice gone silent. Ash hoped he was dead, that he'd died quickly. She couldn't imagine wanting anybody to suffer like that.

Except maybe every single person in Revelation who had served them up as an offering.

A loud banging came from the back of the building. The monster's head turned on a swivel and if Ash had had any room to move, she would have retreated at the sight. Its head was split, folded back along a seam in the middle like the spine of a book. Open to reveal a gaping hole between two suspended pieces of what looked like jawbones or mandibles. The probiscis withdrew, collapsing into the hole and the mandibles joined atop with wet clicks, locking into place, the creature's head more human again, save for the bulging eyes.

It dropped Warren and scurried over the counter, hissing and buzzing. Listening to the sound of the creature retreat, Ash finally allowed herself to cry.

CHAPTER SEVENTEEN

H er eyes were swollen by the time Cal walked carefully back into the main room. She wanted to throw open the lid and run to him, to feel safe, to let someone else be a responsible adult, but she didn't. Just slowly pushed the top open, her body protesting and aching as she freed herself from the confines of the dryer.

A sickly smell gathered at his approach and Ash wrinkled her nose. He winced. "I hid in the trash. I was throwing cans at the other dumpsters. I just wanted to get it out. I saw it fly off and heard screams and. . ." He shuddered.

There wasn't anything to say. Cal rescued people for a living. It had to weigh on him to know what survival suddenly cost.

He swallowed hard. "Where's everybody else?"

Rubbing at her neck, pins and needles in her legs, she shrugged, exhausted.

Charlie and Richie emerged from the bathroom. Charlie's claws were out, dark eyes flashing as she wound her way around the center units and jerked a thumb back in Richie's direction. "This. This right here? Perfect example of why I don't do dick. Do not tell me he is yours. Do not. 'Cause we have fucking standards, and this fails every qualification. He's nasty."

Typical, Ash thought. Someone had just been eaten alive and Richie was trying to get in a pretty girl's pants.

This seemed like a good enough time to end things while she still had a chance. She didn't really feel like dying without an official breakup. Odds were low you were tied to the person you were only dating in the here-after, but they were not zero. "Not mine. I deny ownership."

"Babe—" he began.

"Nope. This is a breakup. Tell your friends I broke up with you in the middle of a life-or-death situation. Play the next girl—or the current!—for sympathy if you live to try your luck."

Richie sneered, but Ash could tell he was embarrassed. "You're such a bitch."

She fluttered her lashes. "The bitchiest."

Eileen slipped slowly back into the room having hidden in a broom closet. She had a death grip on a mop handle, the metal end where it attached to the head dangling freely. "Did y'all see that thing? What it did? I am too old for this shit."

Cal took stock. "Warren?"

"Behind the counter," Ash answered, throat bobbing.

Cal, Charlie, and Richie slipped towards the counter. Eileen moved closer to Ash; they didn't need to see any more. Cal rounded the corner his face drained of color.

Richie wound both hands behind his head. "What the *actual* fuck?"

"It ate him," Ash tried to explain. "It's face just sort of peeled apart. Opened up and this thing shot out—a probiscis. It had to be. And it just sucked him down like a milkshake."

"He looks like a husk," Charlie said, voice quavering. "All dried up and hollow."

Richie bolted for the bathroom, hand over his mouth.

Cal swallowed dryly. "Let's start figuring out what we need to do to get out of here."

Ash pulled out her cheerful map of the town—a mockery of the Hell it had become—and spread it open across the top of one of the tables. She worried her lip and studied the colorful art, the dancing cicada waving from the corner. Taunting her. With a pen she'd found on the desk, she scratched out its stupid googly eyes.

"You doing okay?" Cal asked.

She threw him a withering look. Nobody was okay. "Just would really like to hit something. And Richie doesn't count. He's not worth breaking my hand over. Bitch, not stupid."

"Well, if I had to be on a survival team with a sweet girl or a bitch, I'll take the bitch every time."

She didn't have it in her to smile just then, but she hoped he knew how much she appreciated it. The rest of their slowly diminishing group joined them, Richie emerging from the bathroom looking a little green.

Ash pointed at the map. "There's enough cars packed into the lot that if we set fuses, they would either have to bring the truck down here or risk losing half their town."

"Wouldn't that be like a huge bomb or something?" Richie asked. "They'd see that shit for miles!"

Cal grunted. "That's only in the movies. Cars don't exactly blow up just because you light a tank on fire, but so many packed together would give us a good chance of taking the laundromat at the very least."

"Lots of chemicals in that broom closet," Eileen said. "Most of 'em with warning labels."

"There's still the same problem I had with the promised fireworks." He gestured to the forest surrounding the town. "This whole area is a tinderbox. One major road in and out. Wind shifts, and we're walking through a tunnel of fire. They aren't going to just let us leave."

"So we go into the trees," Charlie offered.

"That's where that thing came from," Ash pointed out.

Charlie gave her a look as if to say she wasn't an idiot. "But how far in? That is a massive bug and has a wingspan of what? Eight feet? No way it can fly through a dense forest easily. A lot of the trees in this area are conifer and allelopathic, dropping needles that don't allow for too much vegetation to grow too close. They protect themselves from being suffocated. So, more room to move around when you molt if the tree you're parking yourself on is smothering everything else around it. And here," she swept her finger across the forest on Ash's map, "is a ravine. Only a couple of miles in. We'd have to book it. But if we can get to that and down, we should be okay."

"How do you know all this?" Ash asked.

Charlie smiled that dazzling smile Ash had first seen her use on the street that afternoon in front of the camera. "That's why I'm here. I do eco content on TikTok, but I'm in the area doing research for my thesis in forestry: 'Social Responsibility and Forest Etiquette: Humanity as Invasive Pest and the Vanishing of the Southeastern Conifer Forests'." She paused. "I may have to update my findings after this."

"Oh my God," Ash snorted. Charlie elbowed her in the ribs.

Beside them, Cal scratched at his jaw, the five o'clock shadow of stubble he had growing in crackling against his nails. "If the fire spreads to the trees, and it likely will, it might not burn too hot too fast with all the rotting vegetation and the humidity out there, but it is going to suck plenty of moisture out of the air. I don't know how deep the ravine is, but even if we're clear of the smoke, it could be difficult to breathe.

"But it's still our best bet," he conceded. He pointed to where Ash had stumbled out of the wood. "That tour path. We take that route into the trees, but we head off toward the ravine. Each of those stupid handheld cameras has the night vision option, which will at least help keep us from breaking our necks."

"I've got a compass," Charlie added, pulling it from her pocket. "A real one."

Cal rubbed at his eyes. "Yeah. I'll get those garlands from the posts and set the fuses. They'll burn fast, but I don't really have a better idea right now. Eileen, you start dragging bottles out of the closet. If it says flammable, open it up and dump it everywhere."

"Hell, I'm opening it even if it *doesn't* say flammable."

"The three of you," he said to Ash, Charlie, and Richie, "head to the hardware store. We need flashlights, weapons, anything you think might be useful."

Richie sneered. "What? No way. You want us to cross the street while you just take a stroll through the park and grandma twists the caps off detergent bottles? What if her arthritis acts up?"

Eileen walked right up to Richie and propped her mop handle under his chin. "I will whoop your ass so fast, skinny little matchstick. I have an exercising heart rate of only about ninety beats per minute, so I won't even break a damn sweat before you're crying for your mama, and she probably stopped taking your calls a long time ago."

"I like her," Charlie said, smiling at Ash. "I like her so much."

"Enough," Cal interjected. "Richie, you have to go to unlock doors."

Ash tried not to bristle at having Richie tag along, but she guessed they really did need all hands-on deck if they were going to get out of a town designed to keep them. Not only keep them but kill them.

* * *

"I hate everything about this, just so we're clear," Charlie whispered as they slunk around the back of the building. Thankfully, the sun had gone down behind the trees, casting everything into long shadow. The streetlights had yet to come on, so at least they had one small advantage.

Unless the bug could see in the dark.

They were probably going to die.

"Jesus," Richie mumbled as they rounded the corner. His reaction was, in Ash's humble opinion, an understatement.

Cars smashed together, taillights winking on and off in the growing dark. Tents in the park that had sagged and fallen after the stampede. But it was the bodies they couldn't ignore. Several—too many—had been run down in the street trying to escape, hit by cars speeding too fast down a too narrow road. Some lay in splashes of crimson black, smashed and broken, dropped from a dizzying height onto windshields or asphalt. But others were like Warren: dried husks displaying masks of horror, a few still clutching those stupid cameras.

The thought had Ash holding up her own handheld and pressing record, sweeping the lens across the lot.

"How many do you think there are?" Cal asked.

Whether he meant bodies or bugs, Ash didn't know. One was too many of either.

Far off past the entrance of town came the intermittent sound of gunfire. Closer still, screams and that horrible buzzing. Ash knew her heart could not be the only one racing as they inched along the wall, trying to keep their steps light. A barrier had been dragged into the street at the far end of town. Cars that had tried to get out had ended up smashing into it and then each other, leaving a tangled heap of twisted metal.

She couldn't see the cicada, but she could hear it,

buzzing in her skull and threatening to drive her mad. She tried to focus on the hardware store, a steel gate down over the entrance. She counted up from the corner, knowing they'd have to sneak through the back again, praying there weren't any better locks there than the laundromat had.

"Good luck," Cal whispered, heading into the park to gather the garlands he would need for fuses, ducking down and army crawling between cars and the dead. Ash shivered.

Charlie gave herself a shake, the beads in her hair clicking quietly. "Ok. Let's go."

"Wait a second," Ash said, holding a hand up.

"For what?" Richie grunted.

The roar of the cicada amplified and there was a terrified scream. "For that," Ash said, moving out onto the sidewalk, body bent nearly in half as she tried her best to keep low and out of sight, moving in between cars. Was she proud of using the bug's feeding as a distraction? No, but she would go over the guilt later in therapy. After this, she was going to need so much therapy.

Did her insurance cover therapy? As she stepped over a bloodied corpse, playful bug antenna twisted and tangled on a crushed skull, she decided out-of-pocket was fine.

The shadows weren't as dark on the far side of the street, the tree line further out, pushed back by the long row of residential houses that broke off from the park. All their lights were dark, and Ash knew them only as rectangular shadows, their wraparound porches turned to toothy grins. She imagined the locals inside their safe-guarded homes or in an underground bunker. The damn Rotary Club probably turned it into a potluck. Fuckers.

But Ash was a bitch and bitches didn't subscribe to being the bigger person, just bigger bitches.

She was going to make Revelation pay.

CHAPTER EIGHTEEN

"I need a damn light! I keep hitting the pin." Richie tried for the umpteenth time to break into the back door, pocket-knife out as Ash winced at each scrape and *click* as he tried to find the space where the door met the frame.

"You're already ringing the dinner bell with the noise," Ash reminded him, trying to peer into the darkness.

Richie mumbled something unkind under his breath, but she heard the hiss of the knife as it slid down and then the clunk of the handle turning. The door swung outward, revealing a deeper darkness within. Under normal circumstances, this might have given them pause, but since there was nothing normal about the universe anymore, what was one more roll of the dice? They slipped inside, pulling the door nearly shut behind them. Charlie pressed the flashlight button on her phone till they stood in a small halo of light.

"Charlie, can you start getting the stuff we need? And a couple of those jug bug sprayer things? We'll be right back."

"What?" Richie asked, incredulous.

"We're going next door. The video store. They had all these boxes of tapes in the back. I bet it is the *real* movie. We're taking some with us as proof. We're not going to let these people get away with this again."

"Ash," Charlie said, sounding skeptical. "I get you want to get evidence, but if we just get out we can tell people..."

"And have it turn into a conspiracy theory like Warren said? Be laughed at about the giant bug? No! They lured us here to feed their god or whatever and make their little snuff films! If we have just a few of those tapes, we'll be able to show what happened. Why do you think I'm still carrying this fucking thing?" She held up the VHS recorder slung across her body. "I want the director's cut of this shitshow. And what if—I don't know—those victims or whatever can be identified by those tapes? You heard what Warren said. They were real people!"

Charlie lowered her voice. "You're right. Just... be quick, okay? This feels very Scooby Doo and don't split up gang. I don't like this."

Neither did Ash.

* * *

Back outside, it was more of Richie's whispered grumbling as he tried to break into the video store. Fortunately, either his hands or his brain had sharpened since his last success and Ash was grateful for small favors. Unfortunately, the door squeaked on its hinges when Richie opened it too wide.

They hurried in, hoping the noise hadn't attracted the notice of the monster still out hunting somewhere in the vicinity.

Ash felt along the wall till she reached the beaded curtain, listening to them shift with her touch. The boxes had been just inside. Up high. "Help," she whispered. "Get your phone out. I can't see." A sigh in the dark before Richie's phone light winked on right in her face, making her recoil. "Up there," she pointed as the stars cleared from her vision.

Richie joined her behind the curtain, his light illuminating the boxes she'd seen earlier. Climbing up onto a small table, Ash reached up and passed the first box down. *CICADA UNCUT*. Inside, just as she'd hoped, was one of the tiny VHS-C tapes in a plastic bag and a bunch of VHS tapes all labeled the same as the box. Bingo.

She snatched up the bag, pulling her pack around and shoving it inside. Just one more thing.

Tugging her own phone out of her pocket, she lit her way back out into the greater store, jogging to the counter and the merchandise wall. She took one of the boxed VHS tapes down from the racks, but it was too difficult to cram it into her bag while holding her phone, so she had to stoop behind the counter, placing the phone on the floor, light down. The smell of decades old carpet packed with dust and dirt filling her nose.

From the back of the store, Richie was getting antsy. "Time to go now," he urged, just a floating light somewhere in the back of the room. Then the door opened with a squeal and a beam of light bounced off the wall.

"Oh, I'm so glad you're still with us, son."

The voice of the sheriff had Ash freezing like a deer caught in headlights. But the resounding crack and startled cry from Richie that followed it had her scooting backwards, pulling her things along with her. She heard the curtain of beads go mad and a yelp of surprise before a crash. The lights sprang on overhead and Ash held her breath.

"Yep. You're one I'm glad to see still kickin'," the sheriff said, that lazy drawl right before the sound of one of those heavy boots colliding with what she could only assume was part of Richie's anatomy based on the squealing sound he made. There was a rustling and the sound of those beads falling to the ground like ping-pong balls, *clickity-clacking* across the floor.

"Normally," the officer said, slowly as if thinking it over, "the boys and I do our part out there on the road. Sending the rats back, if you'll pardon the expression. But you just rubbed me the wrong way. Ran your plates. Now, that might come back to haunt me when you turn up missin' like the rest of 'em, but we'll sort it out. We always do. Drive your cars well out of town, do a little shopping on your cards, and make sure some grainy security footage catches someone that looks enough like you to ease minds. But you, son? I just knew you were gonna be a problem with that record. I thought you might try to hole up and I'd have to flush you out like a badger. Had to set a few loose in the street outside just so I could get a look see."

There was another yelp and the sound of something being dragged along the floor. Ash dared to turn her head to follow the sound, shoulders rounding to make herself as small as possible. And there was the bat. Right there. A scuffed, aluminum bat with a taped grip. Tucked back under the edge where it had probably sat for years.

"Hey, man," Richie pled. "You don't want to do this."

"Oh, that depends on what we're talkin' 'bout, really. Do I want y'all comin' into our nice little town with your attitudes and smart mouths? Not really. Do I like the work—and you cannot imagine the work, son—we have to do in order to keep ourselves safe? Of course not. I don't *want* any of that. But it doesn't matter what I want. That's how it's done. That's tradition. And we take traditions very seriously. Loyal to 'em. Loyal to it. Loyalty. Something I bet you don't know much about."

Hard agree, Ash thought.

"But something I do *like*, is making sure little good for nothin' shits like you serve a greater purpose. Something bigger than yourself. Now I'll readily admit—because I'm man enough to do so—that we make mistakes and sometimes there are accidents. And we do feel bad about those. I remember every one. Days like today, when so many of y'all ended up here 'cause of all the business on the 22? Bound to have been mistakes. And I'll repent for those. We all will. But you. You, son? I'm glad you're here."

As Ash's fingers closed round the bat, Richie began blubbering. "No! No! Ple—"

A whistle as something heavy sailed through the air followed by a crunching impact. Over and over. The sheriff was breathing heavy through what sounded like gritted teeth; hard, angry, in and out. He was beating Richie. Only true fear of being discovered kept Ash's eyes clear and hands steady as she pulled the bat from its place and drew it to her before crawling out.

The sheriff was turned away, standing with his arms at his side looking down at Richie twisting pitifully on the ground. His face was a mess of blood and bruises, bright red under the overhead lights. In the officer's hand was his pistol, gloved fingers wrapped round the barrel. She wondered why he hadn't just shot him, but then remembered that the locals weren't the only monster in town. And they were just as afraid of the cicada as the rest of them.

Ash eyed the back door. She wasn't proud of it, but she did.

Dammit. She wasn't completely heartless.

Nope, she thought as she began moving silently at a crouch toward the first shelves. *Just stupid. Stupid, stupid, stupid.*

The sheriff put his hands on his hips and huffed long. "Whew!" He chuckled. "I am out of shape. Used to be I could whup a punk like you without breaking a sweat. Pauly'll be gettin' my job before I know it." He laughed to himself.

Out of the corner of her eye, Ash saw the rack of Disney VHS tapes and thought about that movie with the superhero family with the ginger villain. *You got me monologuing!* The sheriff struck her as the type of mansplainer who loved a monologue.

She rounded the next rack, getting closer.

The officer crouched next to Richie, elbow on his knee, cradling his face with one hand. He placed the gun on the ground next to his feet, streaks of blood shiny on the grip and Ash had to swallow back her revulsion. Richie continued to mumble, words unintelligible.

"No, no, no," the officer said, shaking his head. His uniform shirt was plastered to his back with sweat trickling down his tan neck, his starched collar long-wilted and soaked through. "Don't try to talk. You lost a few teeth there. Now, I expect you want to know what's gonna happen. And I don't mind tellin' you. I'm gonna drag your sorry ass out to the street for the cicada. The buzzards'll get whatever's left. Circle of life and all that."

He stood with a grunt, hands against his lower back as his bones creaked and cracked. "Yep. Pauly'll be gettin' this job sooner than I'd like."

Right behind him, bat high, Ash agreed. "Yep. Way sooner."

CHAPTER NINETEEN

It felt good to hit something.

It also hurt really bad.

She had expected the bat to connect with the Sheriff's temple with a deafening crack. Instead, it was the tinny hum of aluminum and a thud, the sound of a skull fracturing muffled between the thin layers of scalp and the cushion of brain. But the reverberation traveled up the length of the bat and Ash's arms, her already tense muscles screaming in protest at the sudden shock.

It did not, however, stop her from coming around again, the end of the bat arching up to catch under the officer's jaw. His teeth clacking together was more the sound she had been looking for, as was the feeling of give as she shattered bone. She hoped he ate through a straw for the rest of his life just like his fucking pet bug.

As he crumpled to the ground like a broken doll, body limp, blood gushing from between broken teeth and torn lips, Ash highly doubted he would live long enough to pop down to the Piggly Wiggly for an Ensure.

The backdoor squealed and Ash braced herself for the rush of reinforcements. But it was Charlie, shoulders sagging and back bent under the weight of backpacks and the two sprayers she was holding, their contents sloshing inside. She took one look and skidded to a stop, eyes taking in the scene.

"Shit."

Arms shaking, Ash kicked the gun toward Charlie and nudged the fallen officer's foot, but he didn't move. Didn't even moan. Stepping over him, she went to Richie, stooped and cringed. The sheriff had done some serious damage. Orbital socket cracked, nose broken, shattered front teeth. He would not be pretty for a while. But he'd heal.

If they could get out.

"It's okay, Richie," she soothed. Leaning forward, she managed to get up under his arm, lifting him to his feet as he made whimpering noises and leaned heavily on her.

"'Umb 'ick 'ock," he tried, tongue fumbling for words in his broken mouth, blood and drool dribbling onto his stained shirt and pants.

"Can you walk?"

In answer, Richie moaned, managing a staggering line toward Charlie while Ash collected the bat. "At least he gave us a parting gift," Charlie said, stowing the gun in the back of her shorts.

Ash gestured to the wall of *CICADA* merchandise. "Want a souvenir?"

"Pfft," Charlie sputtered. "Pass. Here." She passed one of the laden backpacks to Ash. "Flashlights, those handheld garden shears, headlamps, water. You get what you wanted?"

"Yeah, I think so."

"Oop ee oo," Richie whined, throwing a jazz hand.

"I'm sorry, Richie. We'll get you to a hospital as soon as we can," she promised.

"Can you carry one of these?" Charlie asked him, holding out the smaller of the jug sprayers. "We'll give it to the others as soon as we get back."

A shrug was the only answer they got. Charlie helped him drape the strap over his shoulder.

"Let's go," Charlie nodded toward the door. "And I left some gifts of my own outside."

Ash gestured for her to lead the way, but as they started for the door, both women paused, staring at the walls of VHS tapes surrounding them.. So many screaming women on the covers....

They shared a look.

"Know how every time the girl walks away from 'the body' it gets back up?" Charlie asked.

Ash blew out a breath. "Yeah."

Pivoting, she went back to the Sheriff, squared her hips like a golfer, and took one more swing on the opposite side of his skull. The snap of his neck was audible, blood spraying, teeth flying from his mouth to skitter across the carpeted floor, the only other sound his breath escaping on a last sigh.

"That a girl," Charlie cheered flatly.

Ash wiped away the bit of scalp on his uniform, hair and meat still clinging to the metal.

* * *

Back outside, they found the 'gifts' Charlie had prepared.

"Is this a Molotov cocktail?" Ash whispered as Charlie passed her the bottle.

"As good of one as I could make having no real idea what I was doing, yes. I dumped everything I could find in there on the way out. True bugs, like cicadas, are drawn to light sources. It should offer us some extra cover and, at the very least, fuck this town."

"'imme at," Richie blubbered, snatching the bottle from Ash's hand as he fished his lighter from his pocket. She didn't protest. If she'd had her face caved in, she'd be in a foul mood too. There was the clicking sound of the lighter being struck, a flame, and Richie held it to the soaked rag. It flared bright and orange, the smell of burning chemical strong in their nostrils. Winding up, Richie tossed the homemade grenade into the video store while Charlie did the same in the hardware store. Already primed, the inside of the hardware store flared with an audible *whoosh*, fire rushing across the floor and up shelves like it had intent.

Ash guessed it was arson, but there was no way they'd be charged. She'd laugh her ass off once Revelation's 'council' or whatever had their mugshots all over the news and she was serving them with a gazillion dollar class action lawsuit for damages.

They moved as quickly and as quietly as they could back round the corner, halting almost immediately. The streetlights, dark before, now shone all up and down the street and through the park. All of Revelation lit by spotlights. Here and there, Ash could see figures darting to and fro. Probably the survivors the cop had let go as cover.

The chainsaw buzz of the cicada became a roar, dropping down low over the park, chasing those shifting shadows. How many people could that thing consume? More screams came from the dark and Ash began to lose her nerve. "We're gonna be out in the open."

"Nothing for it," Charlie mumbled quietly at her elbow. "We've got to get across the street. You smell that?"

Ash did. The fire they'd set was already growing. Smoke began to drift by, tickling Ash's throat, begging her to cough. Somewhere, glass shattered. Had to be the stores, the heat looking for escape. *It has to be now*, she thought.

Without warning, she ran forward, into the smoke, cursing inwardly as her shadow fell long in all directions, caught in too many lights. She danced again around cars and the fallen, her only goal the other side of the street. Richie's and Charlie's shadows appeared alongside hers, peculiar flowers blooming on asphalt sprinkled with broken glass and shattered plastic from taillights.

The crackling roar preceded the black shadow that came directly from the park, aiming for them. "Down!" Charlie yelled, the three of them dropping around two abandoned vehicles, bumpers kissing. The bug made a low pass and then swept up again, likely trying to keep clear of the smoke already pouring out from under the steel gates and into the night air.

"Christ," Ash coughed, head up, waiting for the bug to show itself again, but between the smoke and the too-bright streetlights, her eyes were watering. They had to keep going. Better in a group or one at a time? Better to play dead till it passed? She didn't know.

The cicada made the decision for them, diving so fast and low Charlie barely had a chance to scream before the bug's legs snagged on her backpack.

It was revolting, its wings moving too fast for Ash's eyes to follow as it beat back the smoke and tried to gain lift with an unsteady grip on its prey. "Let go of her!" Ash screamed, jumping to her feet and swinging wide with the bat. She clipped a wing along the edge, feeling something more substantial than the wafer-thin membranes. And it was enough of a shock for the creature to slip off the pack, buzzing and sputtering, its rattle angry as it danced back through the air, weaving more to one side, struggling.

Ash reached down and grabbed Charlie up, urging her to her feet. Charlie gave a cry, stumbling along.

"Go, go, go!" Ash shoved her towards a sedan, one rear door open wide as the creature made another sweep of the street. Charlie hurled herself inside and over the backseat leaving streaks of blood that looked black on the gray upholstery. Ash jumped in behind her, pulling the door shut. Charlie was on the floor behind the passenger seat, whimpering as she pulled pieces of red plastic from busted taillights out of her knees, her fingers wet with blood.

"Oh God, where's Richie!" Ash gasped, twisting her head round and round.

She saw his sprayer next to a Jeep Wrangler, its cage crumpled and broken, tires flat. It looked like it had taken a roll or two, likely trying to drive over the side-walks. The air bags were deployed, red across one. She hoped the passenger and driver had walked away with little more than a broken nose and whiplash, though she suspected they'd been carried off like so many others.

Squinting, she could just make out a skinny shadow beneath the body of the car, lying flat on the road. Richie. The cicada circled round and round, the smoke hindering its hunt. But it landed on top of the Jeep, those roll bars a perfect perch. Its thorax twitched and rattled, and its red eyes rolled round in its head.

Ash held up her hands, motioning for him to stay still. She hoped he could see her. *Stay*, she mouthed, over and over. *Stay.*

He gave a weak thumbs up.

"We've got to get out of here," Charlie groaned, pulling another glittering piece of plastic from her flesh. A stack of unused, drive-thru napkins was on the front seat and Ash grabbed for them so Charlie could sop up some of the blood.

"I'm taking suggestions," Ash whispered, staying low behind the seat, hoping all the smoke drifting by obscured the bug's view. "Will it fly higher to avoid the smoke?"

"It should. But *it* shouldn't even *be* to begin with so what do I know. Where is it?"

"It's—"

But it wasn't. It was no longer perched atop the Wrangler, though Richie was still and quiet below. Ash licked bone-dry lips, her tongue scratching across their scabbed surface with the sound of scraping sandpaper.

Where had it gone? The buzzing was still loud, even while the fire raged behind, sucking oxygen with a roar.

Ash's breath hitched.

The rear windshield exploded and both girls screamed. Charlie was tangled in a heap on the floor, legs up on the seat, backpack caught behind her. She kicked out and thrashed as the creature tried to fit its bizarre head through the hole.

"GO AWAY!" The cry tore from Ash's throat and she gave a shallow swing of the bat, her grip choked so high she almost knocked out the side window with the handle. She knocked its skittering legs, pinning one against the edge of the window, glass shards still caught in the frame. The bug squealed and buzzed even louder. Ash bore down, gritting her teeth, hoping its branch-like leg might crack at the joint.

But it was one better. It broke off instead.

The cicada pulled back and smoke poured in through the broken window. Ash inhaled too deep, too fast, throat and lungs burning. It was like she'd taken a drag on her first hundred cigarettes all at once. Coughing and hacking, she reached for Charlie, trying to help her up.

The bug was back, however, with a vengeance. It tore at the remaining glass with its hooked feet, pulling it away in spiderwebbed sheets like peeling an onion back. Ash took up the bat again, holding it over her shoulder and ramming it at whatever part she could reach: feet, legs, an exposed side as it maneuvered.

It exposed the white of its belly as the last of the glass fell away and there was a faint *click* and then an explosion of light and sound. Beside her, Charlie had the Sheriff's gun out and was firing out the window. Ash saw at least two bullets impact the bottom of the thorax before the creature buzzed and scrambled off the trunk. Charlie kept firing, the sound deafening Ash till she could only hear a high ringing. Finally, there were no more bullets and Charlie was just depressing the trigger again and again. But the cicada flew off, nonetheless.

Now was their chance.

Ash scrambled for Charlie's door handle, reaching across her, and shoving her hard. "Come on! Richie!" she screamed as they landed in the road. "Move your ass!"

Richie was already crawling from under the car, hauling the sprayer up and skirting around a shattered hood, slamming the jug of spray into the cracked grill, bouncing right off the hood and only just managing to keep his feet. He kept going.

"He's gonna make it," Charlie said, rounding another car.

No, he wasn't, Ash realized.

The bug was circling again, lower this time. Richie had to have heard and tried to orient himself toward the source of danger with only one good eye. He began priming the pump on the sprayer, ready to release a cascade of poison at the creature if it did come for him. But even in all the commotion, Ash could see it was too easy. The plastic jug holding the liquid had been pierced, the vacuum compromised. Richie might as well have been jerking off for all the good he was doing. Above them, silhouetted against the smoke, the cicada whizzed back and forth, preparing for its next attack.

"Richie! Get down!" she yelled, running toward him, bat in hand.

Finally realizing the futility of his plan, he dropped the plastic container and came barreling back toward Ash. He grabbed her in a hug and her first instinct was to hug him back, to share their terror. It felt almost good.

Until Richie spun her around, arm cranked around her neck. Her hands went to his arm, dropping the bat in surprise.

"Here!" he called, the first clear word she'd heard him speak since the beating she'd saved his ass from! "'Ave 'er!"

"Richie!" Ash choked. Unbelievable. Truly. He was using her as a human shield because she'd dumped his ass.

Okay, that gave him too much credit. He was just a damn coward.

He was also stupid.

Ash wanted to tense up but forced herself to become dead weight and go limp instead. Richie's slight build and already precarious equilibrium had them falling. Releasing the vice grip she had on his arm, Ash covered her face right before they landed on the street, Richie's full weight slamming down on top of her.

He scrambled, trying to get up, but she hooked her leg between his and rolled, giving herself wiggle room. Hauling back, she slammed the heel of her hand into his bleeding mouth and nose, scraping her palm on his broken teeth, making him wail.

He scowled with his one good eye, reaching for her throat. "'Oo 'azy 'itz! I—"

The needle-like tip of the cicada's probiscis popped out of Richie's mouth, stopping only inches from Ash's face. Shocked babbles erupted from Richie's throat and his hands hovered around the probiscis, too afraid to touch it for fear of doing more harm. But Ash could see what Richie could not.

Mandibles, jagged and covered with stiff hairs, gripped the back of Richie's head on either side. The creature's face—if she could call it that—was pressed close. A thick stream of hot blood and fluids poured from Richie's open mouth, some dripping off the end of the probiscis. The cicada had punctured a hole through the back of Richie's head, straight through his skull. Spindly legs wrapped round his torso and the mandibles closed down. Richie looked at her, pleading, scared. She tried to say his name. She hadn't wanted this, even after what he'd done.

Richie was pulled backwards and up into the air, like he had been sucked up into a tornado. The death rattle of the creature fading into the black above as it carried Richie away to feast in peace.

Ash scrambled up, breath coming out in ragged sobs and choked screams. She struggled to find her balance with the backpack, but she managed to stay upright as Charlie appeared, tugging her hand.

"Come on." No platitudes. No questions. They didn't have time for those things.

Shoving one more trauma down into the pit of her stomach, Ash knelt for the bat and followed Charlie as she disappeared back into the parking lot.

CHAPTER TWENTY

The chemical smell was enough to make Ash gag as they opened the back door to the laundromat. She might never do laundry again, the scents of Tide and disinfectant permeating the air even through the second door.

Cal and Eileen were there, waiting. Eileen still had her mop handle and Cal had his own backpack. "We were getting worried," he said with relief as Ash and Charlie entered, faces and arms glistening with sweat. He looked them both up and down, noticed the marks on Ash's face and arms. "What happened? Where's Richie?"

Ash didn't have the words, but Charlie had her covered. "In Hell."

"Are we ready?" Ash choked out, hands clenched so hard her nails were digging into her palms.

Cal blinked his surprise. "Uh, yeah. Yeah. We just have to light the fuses here."

Ash pulled the lighter she'd bought in the gas station out of her pocket, the dancing cicada on the pink background. Cal gestured to the fuse he'd laid through the gap in the door into the larger room using the lengths of garland and some fibrous rope material. "Be my guest. Charlie, open the door and everybody be ready to run. Straight back to the tree line." He picked up a handmade torch fashioned from a broken broom handle and soaked rags, probably from the supply closet. "I'll light the lot."

"Remember," Charlie said, handing out headlamps, "bugs are drawn to light. We should be fine once we're in the trees. But we don't want to risk lights too early, so it is gonna be dark. Be fast, but be careful."

Ash took in their ragtag group. Headlamps, clothes disheveled, wielding sprayers, mop handles, and baseball bats and looking like something out of an apocalyptic horror film.

Oh, right.

As she struck the lighter and bent to light the fuse, Ash promised, "First round is on me when we get back to civilization." There was a hissing pop as the garland lit, smoldering for a moment before finally catching. The little flame traveled through the tightly woven reeds and grasses, the tiny, crafted insects shriveling as they were consumed. "Good riddance," Ash said, rising to her feet and tossing Cal the lighter.

They fled into the night, Cal flicking the *BIC* till it caught. His homemade torch whooshed to life, drenched as it was. He sprinted into the lot, dropping the torch low and lighting his pre-laid path. Behind them, Ash could hear the inside of the laundromat becoming engulfed while, across the street, Revelation already burned out of control. The fire spread onto the residential street, consuming the well-trimmed lawns and delicate magnolia trees till they were charred, grasping hands, their long fingers reaching for the first houses.

"Go," Cal urged, waving her into the trees as he threw the torch away and ran to catch up, another roar beginning to overtake the sound of the fire.

They kept close to the trees till they hit the path and then in, the air turning cool and fragrant as they fled down the trail. It was exactly as Charlie had warned, the darkness almost all consuming. Soon, their steps were slowing, and Ash was holding her hands out in front of her for fear of running into a tree, toeing the ground and hoping she kept on the path. The only illumination came from Eileen's shoes, the heels blinking in a rainbow of colors with each step.

From somewhere ahead, Charlie's headlamp bloomed, and they gathered close beside her. Her compass in hand, shaking so hard Ash couldn't even begin to see how she could read it.

"We need to head uphill here, through the trees." That meant no more trail. Charlie's lamp moved back and forth as she shook her head. "I don't know how heavy the trees are above us here. They'll thicken up, but I don't know when. We just have to try and stay quiet and hope that thing goes for easier prey."

"Maybe it will follow the road," Eileen said. "Back toward all that gunfire. Bound to be plenty of murderers to eat, right?"

"God, I hope so," Ash croaked as she pulled up her handheld, flipping on the night vision. Charlie turned off her headlamp and did the same.

They plunged into the trees, no longer on packed dirt

but grass and decomposing leaves. Ash truly hoped they were nowhere near any dead-cat-racoons because she was just not in the mood. It was slow going as they tried to follow the strange, greenish light of their screens. It was all a little unreal. Ash felt like her reality was suspended, feeling more like she was playing a virtual reality video game than experiencing real life.

And always the fire, a looming threat behind them, even as they wove deeper and deeper into the forest, trampling through underbrush.

Soon, they were all out of breath, coughing from smoke and exertion and stumbling up hill and down again. The world around them grew lighter and Ash thought it might be dawn. That time worked as backwards as everything else in Revelation. But it was only the fire creeping closer, the smoke a heavy fog around them. And suddenly, Ash couldn't even tell if they were all together.

"Cal?" she called, quietly, her eyes stinging, puffy and angry.

"I'm here," he said, touching her elbow. "Eileen? Charlie?"

A series of hacking coughs. "Here," Charlie croaked from up ahead and a light bloomed, a tiny star in the dark. Her face looked ghoulish in the light thrown by her headlamp. "Where's Miss Eileen?"

Cal and Ash hurried to her, flipping their own lamps on. "Eileen?" How could they have gotten separated? Loathe to lose someone else, especially a sweet someone like Eileen, Ash called louder, voice raspy with smoke. "Eileen!"

Faintly, from somewhere both too far and too close, came a beeping. Eileen's watch. Then a yelp of surprise. A cry cut off and that too familiar crackling thrum of the cicada. A thrashing and the breaking of branches. A screech. And silence.

"Oh, Jesus," Charlie whimpered. "Miss Eileen."

"Goddammit!" Ash bit out. "God-fucking-dammit!"

Cal's headlamp bobbled in the dark. "Pull out the cameras. Just night vision. We need to go as dark as possible. At least for a bit."

"We can't leave her," Charlie pleaded, wiping her running nose on the back of her arm, a silvery streak against her dark skin.

"Nothing we can do," Cal argued, head lamp snapping off. "We have to keep going."

Ash knew he was right and almost hated him for it. Lungs and eyes burning, the scent of ash and smoke heavy in the air, they walked on, holding the camcorders up, the tiny screens glowing shades of green in the dark. She turned at every sound, sure the cicada or some other nightmare creature would come bursting from the trees. But she wasn't alone. Each crack of a branch or rustle in the underbrush had them all on edge.

They walked for what felt like miles. Ash's bare legs covered with stinging scratches, feet aching in her shoes. Blisters formed on her toes, the wet seeping through her socks where several had popped, her blood mixing with pus. Would it draw the creature to them?

"Here," Charlie finally said through silent tears. On her screen, Ash could see where they had left tracks along her pretty face. She'd been crying since they'd lost

Eileen and Ash would have liked to offer her new friend comfort if she had any to spare. "The ravine should be right here. Just ahead. Be careful."

They formed a line, sweeping their cameras from side to side as they looked for the edge that would mark the ravine, inching forward, ever mindful of the glow encroaching along their backs as the fire spread. Ash imagined Charlie felt immense guilt at the destruction. Ash might later.

She hoped there would be a later to feel anything at all.

CHAPTER TWENTY-ONE

"**M**other—"

Charlie's arms pinwheeled, her camera slipping from her grip and falling to the forest floor and rolling away. Down. Ash grabbed for her, hooking fingers in the waistband of Charlie's shorts and hauling her back.

Wheezing, hands pressed over her heart, Charlie gave a humorless laugh. "I found it."

If by found it she meant nearly stepping into thin air and plummeting down the steep side of the ravine over jagged rocks and through thick brambles, she was correct. Maybe not the best way to find something, but you could hardly argue with the results. The ravine stretched into deeper darkness in all directions, including down. The poor quality of the night vision barely illuminated the first few feet of the descent. To Ash, it looked like a black hole in the middle of the forest.

"Down there?" she asked.

Breath and equilibrium regained, Charlie exhaled. "Yeah. It shouldn't be too deep, but we can't climb down holding these." She jiggled her camera. "We'll have to risk the lights."

Ash looked up, aiming her camera lens toward the sky. She didn't even know if there were trees overhead blotting out the stars or if it was the wafting smoke from town. Far behind them, the glow of the flames looked like the sunrise, indicative of how massive the fire had grown. There would not be a single structure not alight by now.

Without a word shared among them, they switched on their headlamps. For Ash, at least, it was the hardest portion of their flight yet. With each inch she slid into the crevice, hand over hand on rock and thick roots, nails broken, hands stinging, she anticipated the ominous clicking and hairy, fiberglass legs to wrap round her torso before she was ripped into space.

But her feet scraped bottom and she collapsed, gasping. The air tasted better down in the gully and while ash still coated her tongue, her lungs inflated with less heat. Charlie took a moment to orient herself and then led the way. They stumbled through the ravine, splashing through shallow water, slipping over pebbles and worn river rocks, and clambering over trees that grew almost horizontal from the sides of the valley, taking only the briefest respites to drink water, for Charlie and Cal to pass the jug of bug killer back and forth, or, in Ash's case, cough up what tasted like tar.

She would never smoke or vape again.

They wandered through the darkness for hours, bodies on autopilot, following the path cut through the forest. Ash's legs became things separate from her, squishy damp in her shoes from puddles of water and blood, the pain dulled to something abstract as exhaustion warred with anticipation. It just couldn't be easy. Nobody just walked away in a horror movie. And that's what they were in: a horror movie.

Worse, she joked inwardly, a horror *sequel*.

"Oh my God," Charlie said ahead of them.

Ash instinctively lifted the bat, the weapon giving her some degree of comfort since they'd descended into the ravine. Her grip cramped on the taped end, and she was pretty confident she'd left indents in the metal. But instead of a scream, she gave an exclamation of disbelief. Just ahead, shining between the trees, was the yellow wash of streetlights.

"Oh my God," Cal echoed, big body sagging. "Thank you."

It took them some time to find a place to ascend the gorge, using a tree's exposed root system to pull themselves up, dirt and grit raining down, bouncing off lights and catching on their lips till they were all spitting soil. But then they were up and half-running, half-falling through the trees toward the lights.

As they grew brighter, Ash slid to a halt and urged the others back. "Wait, wait! Turn off the lights!"

They slipped down to the forest floor, snapping their headlamps off. All Ash wanted to do was lie down and sleep in the cool dirt and leaves, the smell of pine heavy in her nose. But they weren't out of the woods yet.

Hilarious, she thought.

"We don't know if any of the people from Revelation are out there," she said quietly, craning her neck to try and peer through the dark. "What if they're waiting to ambush or something?"

Charlie cursed, butt landing hard in the dirt as she sat.

"We go in slow," Ash said. "Just in case."

"I can go," Cal volunteered. "You two took the bigger risk last time."

"No," Ash snapped with finality. "I'm going." She tightened her grip on the bat. "If I have to take some more heads with me, I'm good with that."

Beside them, Charlie opened her pack and took out a pair of pruning shears. "I'm ready."

"Alright. Slow and quiet. We see what's out there. First sign of anybody, run back this way."

Bent over almost double, they crept through the remaining woods. Ash was conscious of every snap of twig or crack of branch as they walked, half expecting either the monster to come swooping down or flashlights shining in their faces, angry rednecks pursuing them into the dark. Still, even as they left the safety of the tree line, nothing else moved. And Ash knew where they were.

Dottie's gas station, the very place where everything began to go wrong, materialized in the dark ahead, the dusty parking lot and old fuel pumps looking abandoned. The neon sign was dark in the windows, the entire place feeling even more deserted than it had that afternoon.

Had it really been less than a day?

No other lights shone save for a faint red glow in the distance Ash guessed to be Revelation. And it was quiet.

Too quiet.

Ash, so used to the sounds of traffic and city life and, so recently, the relentless hum of the cicadas and screams of those being hunted, found the silence unsettling. She made an 'o' with her lips, breathing in and out as quietly as possible as they tiptoed across the parking lot. They pressed themselves to the side of the building, Charlie cupping her hands against the dusty, grimy window to peer inside. "Nothing."

They made their way to the front door, shaking the handle and hearing the glass rattle in the frame. Locked. Ash had a faint thought that Richie would have been useful, but then she remembered he had tried to feed her to a bug, so fuck Richie.

Better, she decided, to skip straight to the acceptance stage of grief.

Using the bat as a battering ram, she held her breath and slammed the end into the door, wincing at the sound of shattering glass in the clear, empty night.

Behind her, Cal chuckled dryly.

"Bitches get shit done, Cal," she said through gritted teeth as she finally turned the locks inside with clumsy fingers. The door fell open, the bell above startling all of them. They hurried inside, relocking the door and ducking down, sure of pursuit.

They sat on the floor, listening for footsteps on gravel or the sound of an approaching car. Finally, Cal stood slowly to look out the window. "Clear."

"What do we do now?" Ash was finding it hard to stand, calves hard as rocks and her knees screaming in pain, threatening to buckle. Rubbing at her lower back, she wagered she'd aged fifty years since that morning. She probably had gray hairs.

"I want a bathroom," Charlie said using the bug sprayer to leverage herself up.

Ash agreed. She also wanted to wash her face and hands, the sweat and blood combined with the ash and dirt making her feel like she was wearing a disgusting mud mask. Remembering the key Dottie had handed her that morning, Ash stumbled toward the front counter. "There's a key. Hang on."

"It looks like there's a truck round the corner," Cal said. "Maybe there's a spare key inside?"

"First things first," Charlie said, squeezing her legs together and waddling towards the back of the store, still holding the gun.

Unslinging the camcorder from her shoulder, she placed it on the counter, only half noting the red light still recording as she slipped around the corner to look for Dottie's 'The Shitter' hammer. "Cal, could you see if there is any Icy Hot or muscle. . . stuff? Hey, Jerry," she added, patting the taxidermy armadillo on his dusty rump.

Jerry only stared with his wide, blind eyes.

"Me too, Jerry. It's been that kind of day."

Cal had walked deeper into the room but turned at her voice. "Who are you talking—"

The front door exploded inwards.

CHAPTER TWENTY-TWO

Ash had half a heartbeat before she covered her ears with both hands and dropped, the smell of gasoline, dust, and red clay filling her nostrils as she pressed her face to the floor. She'd seen Cal, his body bucking wildly before he fell into a candy display, a spray of glass sparkling like party glitter in the air. The boom was almost secondary, like thunder after a flash of lightning.

Her ears were ringing and she opened her mouth wide, trying to pop them. She could hear Cal moaning and the crunch of boots on glass and then that smoker's cough preceding the tinkling of the bell above the door. It sounded wrong. Too cheerful after such violence.

"I'm always tellin' 'em. Hoodlums. Hoodlums will do the most vile things if they ain't checked right off the bat. I mark 'em and tell 'em right off, but they don't always listen."

Dottie, the cantankerous gas station owner who had put Richie in his place so beautifully that morning, gave a tremendous cough as she entered her store. The truck Cal had seen most likely belonged to her. She had probably been sitting in it, quietly and patiently, watching the road in case anybody got out.

Marked. That's what she'd said about Richie. And she'd told Ash that if she went with him, she deserved whatever she got. She'd assumed the woman meant something like herpes! Dottie was instead Revelation's first and last line of defense, holed up at her waystation somewhere between the civilized world and Hell, ferrying people into town like a beehived Charon.

"I know you're back there, so you just come on out or I fill this one so full of buckshot he'll look like a colander."

Ash writhed on the ground and made to rise, groaning in pain as she got up to her knees, pissed as much as hurt. They had escaped a sadistic town, a monstrous bug, and endured a grueling hike while pursued by fire and she was going to bite it at some Podunk gas station that had a fucking armadillo named Jerry as its conversation piece. Murdered by a geriatric mee-maw! She'd even broken up with Richie and hadn't even had a drink to celebrate!

She was wrong; she was so much more pissed than hurt, her fingers wrapping around the handle of 'The Shitter's' hammer.

Ash stood, arms at her side, and glared over the counter at Dottie, standing among the rubble and broken glass. No tears. No pleading. Nope. Just Ash's perfected Active Bitch Face.

Dottie tsked, blinking behind those enormous glasses, her shotgun dropped just a bit below her shoulder, finger still resting on the trigger guard. "Girl, I tried to warn you. You looked like you had some damn sense. Don't think you're gonna get any sympathy from me."

"Didn't ask for it." Ash said, voice deadpan.

Dottie hacked up a lung as she laughed. "Well, that's true. Now," Dottie shouldered the shotgun again. "Raise your hands slowly."

Ash slowly lifted her left arm, fist curled, middle finger up.

At the same time, she hauled back with her right and sent the hammer flying straight at Dottie's face. Or hair. The hair was a bigger target.

On instinct, Dottie gasped and swung the shotgun, trying to deflect, but too late. The hammer sailed through the air end over end, the heavy end colliding— not with her head or her hair—but her windpipe. Apparently, Ash threw curves.

The gun fell to the ground and Dottie's gnarled hands reached for her throat, gasping and sputtering for air. As the shotgun clattered, Charlie charged forward, a battle cry erupting from her throat, those pruning shears gripped tight in a bloody fist. Her arm arched, stabbing down again and again above Dottie's hip and the clerk's leg buckled.

Ash came round the corner and fell upon the bug sprayer, madder than she'd ever been in her life and nowhere near rational. She grabbed Dottie by that crispy updo, hauled her head back and jammed the spray nozzle down her throat, pressing the trigger and releasing a stream of poison down the woman's gullet.

Dottie flailed and tried to collapse, but Ash showed no mercy, holding her upright by her hair. Only reached down and pumped the sprayer to give it some more juice. Another stream of the liquid swallowed. Ash imagined the burning of Dottie's organs, how she had to be shriveling up from the inside. And it was how Dottie looked, her fingers curling in, arms like a dying bug's.

There was no sympathy in Ash's heart for the woman. Not knowing what she had done. How she had been a sort of Pied Piper, guiding the rats to their death. And how she'd prided herself on the suggestion she had given Ash a choice? Ash did not recall her saying, "Ditch the loser *or* you get eaten." There had been terms and conditions in that morning speech Dottie had conveniently left out.

And then there was that tell-tale rattle, low and thrumming, and the glass burst inwards as the cicada flew inside, its big body crumpling the metal frame of the door like paper. Ash stared at Dottie still mewling and twitching in her grasp.

"Charlie!" Ash screamed, grabbing hold of Dottie's collar.

Ash yanked the nozzle from Dottie's throat as Charlie rushed forward, a puff of air and a gurgling sound escaping with it. The whites of Dottie's eyes showed, turning red and sickly behind her cracked glasses. With a heave, the two women shoved Dottie forward, stumbling backwards into the cicada standing impossibly tall on its back legs to embrace the flailing woman. It's face split with a sucking sound, those mandibles parting. It turned Dottie in its many legs to stand face to face. Ash had the extreme satisfaction of hearing the woman gargle a scream right before the black probiscis shot down

Dottie's throat. The cicada's thorax rattled as it began sucking, drawing in, Dottie's already droopy flesh hollowing, her body eclipsed in the great shadow of the monster.

Ash heard Cal scrambling along the floor and turned to find him reaching for the discarded shotgun. She yanked Charlie back, the girl's face contorted into a mask of horror.

The cicada's body relaxed and then tensed, perhaps taking another draw, but this one was arrested. Dottie's body fell to the ground and the probiscis remained extended, its body contorting. An inhuman scream came from the creature, though it didn't seem to have a mouth to scream with. From between Dottie's parted lips, yellowed foam and bloody bubbles spilled in a stream onto the floor, mixing with the broken glass. Above her fallen form, the cicada danced, a terrible, blood-spattered caricature of the painted bug from Ash's lighter. The strange screams continued to echo in the too tight space, and the cicada tossed its head this way and that, mandibles wide, exposing the bizarre maw and now swollen probiscis, the tube dotted with pus and blood.

There was the cock of the shotgun and Cal raised it high. "Smile you son-of-a—"

A single shot and the bug's head exploded, streams of yellow and green and black spraying through the air to fall in thick, mucusy ropes to the floor. It jolted and jerked and finally fell to its back, spinning across the floor with a whir, white belly shaking in its death throes. Slowly, it began to still, legs twitching, and leaving them with a dead bug the size of a horse.

None of them moved for some time.

It was Charlie who finally broke the silence. "What movie was that line from?"

"*JAWS*," Cal said, breath still coming heavy. "I saw that poster in the store. Been in my head all day."

"Oh."

"Nerd," Ash hiccupped. "Such a nerd."

They helped Cal up, his face and arms littered with tiny glass shards, but nothing tweezers and Advil wouldn't fix. They strode for the door, giving both Dottie and the bug a wide berth. As if on cue, they all paused just outside.

"Hey," Charlie said, pushing her heavy dreads from her shoulder. "Didn't they make like three or four sequels to *JAWS*?"

Goddammit. Ash sighed. "Yeah."

The trio strode back in, shoes pulverizing glass. Cal pawed a couple of shotgun shells from Dottie's pocket while Ash retrieved the bat and Charlie found the hammer.

CHAPTER TWENTY-THREE

Charlie had the decent foresight to fish the truck keys from Dottie's pockets before they made a bigger mess of the station. Ash had taken her bat to every single one of Dottie's *CICADA* tapes. Her arms would be protesting for days.

At least they'd gotten to use the restroom and clean up as best they could. The truck bed reeked of old cigarette smoke (thanks Dottie), sweat, dried blood, and an odor Ash couldn't identify, but she was pretty sure bug guts coated the bottom of her shoes.

"Why did you bring that?" Cal asked from the driver's seat, glancing in her lap.

Ash patted Jerry the armadillo's freshly dusted nose. "Souvenir."

They rolled down the dark road back toward the main highway. In the side mirror, Ash could see the glow of the fires. Now they drove off, the cicada secured in the truck bed like some sort of hunting trophy, the camcorders and precious tapes gathered in the backseat.

Ash took a long breath, the first easy one since the day had started and leaned her head against the cool window. Something winked on and off ahead and she furrowed her brow. At first, she suspected a trauma induced hallucination or maybe a chemical high delusion. But Cal must have seen the same thing since he eased off the gas.

Ash cackled. "You've got to be kidding."

There, on the shoulder of the road, arms pumping, tiny lights winking in and out on her heels, was Eileen. Power walking back toward the highway. Her sweatsuit was caked with mud and her short, gray hair was so littered with pine needles she looked like she had a hedgehog perched on her head. But she was alive.

And booking it.

Charlie rolled down the window. "Miss Eileen, I love you!"

Eileen's mouth twitched, lips pursed as she breathed steadily, eyes straight ahead as they rolled alongside her. "Wondered when y'all would show up. Thought I'd have to walk all the way to 22. And I'd have done it, too!"

"I've no doubt," Ash said, wiping a tear. "But how about you hitch the rest of the way with us?"

Charlie shuffled over and Miss Eileen climbed in the back with a huff. "Mercy," she groaned as the seat enveloped her. Then she wrinkled her nose. "It stinks to high heaven in here. What did y'all step in?"

"Don't ask," Cal said.

It was only minutes before soft snores sounded from the back. Ash turned to see Eileen, head thrown back on the seat, mouth open. Charlie was curled up on the seat beside her, long legs tucked in, and her head cushioned on her backpack. Ash settled in her own seat, absently petting Jerry as they made their way toward the highway.

"So," Cal said, not looking at her. Or maybe just avoiding Jerry's dead eyes. "Assuming we don't end up in jail, is the first round still on you?"

"A drink would be nice," she agreed. "But no ice cream. And no movies."

"Yes, ma'am."

Ash shut her eyes. She really could get used to this.

EPILOGUE

The hiss and hollow whistle of his PAPR was so loud. He'd never seen a fire like this in his ten years. Never thought to, even. He'd had house fires, sure. Occasional homemade meth lab explosions. A chemical fire here and there. That tractor trailer on 22 just yesterday. That had been a mess. But this?

This was California wildfire shit.

They'd had to work forward from town and back from the ravine to keep it contained. Helicopters still moving in and out, the perimeter tightening. They might be able to save most of the forest, but that town? Gone. All of it.

They'd not even had a chance to remove the barricade.

What kind of sick, twisted minds barricaded an entire town inside and set it on fire?

He wasn't sure he wanted to know.

He'd lost sight of Simmons. *Goddammit.* They'd given him a rookie and he'd lost him. No. No. Simmons had lost *him*. That's how he'd play it when he found the little SOB.

His heavy boots crunched along the charred forest floor, whole bushes disintegrating to ash as he brushed against them in his heavy suit and coat. The air was thick with smoke as the fire still raged between him and the town. But nothing else here for the fire to eat, at least. Everything he could see through his goggles was a burned-up match. Full sized trees, saplings, underbrush...

Something cracked under his boot. Looking down, he saw a camcorder. The handheld kind they'd had when he was a kid that used those little VHS tapes. He kicked at it, watching it tumble forward and into a patch of grass, dispelling the ash. It might not have been green, as far as he could tell with the whole world in gray and sepia tones, but it wasn't dead. Just ahead, a trunk with a circumference so wide it would take three or four members of the unit linking hands to make it round. One side was entirely black to about thirty, forty feet up. Beyond was a small grove, the huge conifers still full, their needles dusty with soot, everything covered with a fine layer of ash like gray snow. And something on one of the trees.

"The hell is that?"

His voice was muffled inside the respirator, the words passing over his lips like a cool breeze. But only for a moment before they simply became more moisture, more heat. His shirt, jeans, and underwear were just a second skin, plastered to him with sweat gathering in small puddles inside his boots. The heavy coat and helmet, his pants and gloves, was all heavy and hot. But they did their job keeping him safe. Like armor or that thing bugs had. An exoskeleton?

"The hell is that?" he said again, squinting to see through his goggles.

The mass might have been an oddly shaped tumor. Maybe even a gall. Conifers were prone to both. But it reminded him of something.

He marched into the grove, the sound of his respirator and the swirl of ash putting him in mind of wanting to be an astronaut as a child. Back when he still believed in alien worlds. The growth, too, contributed to this fancy. Its shape both familiar and alien.

He lifted a gloved hand and wiped the fine residue from the mass, surprised to not feel the rough bark of the tree beneath the thick padding, but something smoother. He continued brushing, keeping his touch light, till he had about a square foot cleared, though black streaks remained on the surface.

He cocked his head to the side, marveling at an almost perfectly round bulge he'd revealed.

"Jesus," he said, realizing why it looked so familiar. A cicada's exoskeleton before it molted looked like this. But the size of it. . . He peered in, wondering if his goggles or his brain was fried after so many hours and so much heat. His respirator hissed.

Something inside the dome moved.

He reeled back with a curse, spinning his arms to keep his balance, but failing. His heavy gear took him down and he landed hard, cinders billowing like a cloud, obscuring the growth from his view. In a panic, he scooted back on his butt, away from the tree, closer to the center of the grove, trying to slow his breathing.

As the cloud settled, he could see it again, still as a statue. Maybe he'd imagined it.

He swallowed spit that tasted like sweat and burned pine and tried to stand, ready to go back and radio for Simmons. He needed air. Needed a break.

But as he got to his feet and turned to leave, he noticed similar figures on all the trees. Dust had settled into grooves that looked too much like eye sockets, wings, and thoraxes. He spun in a slow circle, noting the way the growths no longer looked like they had grown from the tree, but had instead perched on it. All of them almost perfect.

Save one. One had cracked right down the middle leaving a deep cavern, both sides peeled apart like for an autopsy.

He took a deep breath, respirator clicking and hissing.

Behind him, he heard a deep rattle.

STOP ■

ACKNOWLEDGMENTS

Sitting down to write acknowledgements feels a lot like I imagine accepting an Oscar would be. Like you'll inevitably forget to thank someone before the orchestra plays you off. But I'm going to try.

I want to thank Alan who has loved my work since the first story I sent to Shortwave. I'm so grateful for all the opportunities Alan has given me and my words, including this one. I've come out of this with an incredible publisher and an even more valuable friendship.

Thank you to Erin Foster for her editing eye and for being so excited to read my weird, bug horror.

To Cortney Radocaj, of course. I loved having you champion my work. Thank you for being the first to ride into publishing with me.

Thanks is due to my powerhouse agent, Marcy Posner, and her incredible assistant Jess Macy. Thank you for inviting me to join your dream team!

To my parents who started me early on books and horror with Mary Downing Hahn, Stephen King, R.L. Stine, and Alvin Schwartz. For taking us to the library every week, moving hundreds of books with us from state to state, and letting me walk down the street to the old video store so I could rent obscure horror films. I should also thank you for returning to Mississippi so I'd be forced to drive I-22 during the height of cicada season.

Thank you to my bestie-best, Chris Stoneley, for every bougie coffee, every word of encouragement, and for never failing to surprise me. Thank you for being my always best friend.

I cannot adequately express my gratitude to my writing coven—Rae Wilde, Thea Lyons, Amanda Casile, & Jessica Mitacek—for their constant support, guidance, and cheerleading. Thank you for sharing your words and friendship with me. I love y'all.

A special thanks to my Hobbits for thinking their mom is famous and cool. One day you will know the truth, but this is nice.

And a forever thank you to Doug. For being the first to read this book and laughing through the whole thing (in a good way). For being so supportive of all my crazy dreams and crazier ideas. For better and for worse. I love you.

ABOUT THE AUTHOR

Tanya Pell's short fiction can be found in *Mother Knows Best*, *OBSOLESCENCE*, *Shortwave Magazine*, and *Well, This is Tense*. Find her at tanyapell.com.

A NOTE FROM SHORTWAVE

Thank you for reading the fourth Killer VHS Series book! If you enjoyed *Cicada*, please consider writing a review. Reviews help readers find more titles they may enjoy, and that helps us continue to publish titles like this.

For more Shortwave titles, visit us online...

OUR WEBSITE

shortwavepublishing.com

SOCIAL MEDIA

@ShortwaveBooks

EMAIL US

contact@shortwavepublishing.com

ALSO AVAILABLE FROM SHORTWAVE PUBLISHING

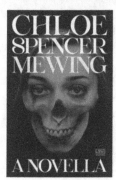

ALSO AVAILABLE
FROM
SHORTWAVE PUBLISHING

ALSO AVAILABLE
FROM
SHORTWAVE PUBLISHING

ALSO AVAILABLE
FROM
SHORTWAVE PUBLISHING

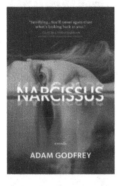

ALSO AVAILABLE
FROM
SHORTWAVE PUBLISHING

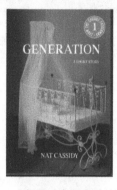

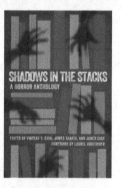

CHAPMAN CHAPBOOKS

CLAY McLEOD CHAPMAN

A series of chapbooks featuring original short stories by Clay McLeod Chapman.

Availabel Titles:

"Mama Bird" is the dark and unsettling tale of a young picky eater and the mother willing to do anything to feed her child.

"Baby Carrots" is the story of a man haunted by a bad batch of produce.

"Knockoffs" are popping up everywhere. Online, on vacation, and—soon—on your block!

FROM THE CASSIDY CATACOMBS

NAT CASSIDY

A series of chapbooks featuring original short stories by Nat Cassidy.

"Generation" · When expecting a new baby, it's normal to have questions. What will my baby look like? What if I'm not ready? What if it's not human? What if this is happening all over? What if this is the end of the world? When expecting a new baby, it's normal to be scared.

Also Available:

"The Art of What You Want"

SHADOWS IN THE STACKS

VINCENT V. CAVA, JAMES SABATA, and JARED SAGE

Shadows in the Stacks is a new horror anthology, published in co-operation with Spirited Giving, to benefit the Library Foundation SD.

Shadows in the Stacks features all-new horror stroies from Clay McLeod Chapman, Jamie Flanagan, Ai Jiang, Jonathan Maberry, Tim McGregor, and more...

Printed in the USA
CPSIA information can be obtained
at www.ICGtesting.com
LVHW032052300924
792531LV00008B/448

9 781959 565345